Also by Michelle Gordon:

Earth Angel Series:

The Earth Angel Training Academy

The Earth Angel Awakening

The Other Side

The Twin Flame Reunion

The Twin Flame Retreat

Visionary Collection:

Heaven dot com

The Doorway to PAM

The Elphite

I'm Here

Oracle Cards:

Aria's Oracle

Velvet's Oracle

Amethyst's Oracle

The Twin Flame Resurrection

Michelle Gordon

theamethystangel.com

All rights reserved; no part of this book may be reproduced, stored in a retrieval system, or transmitted, in any form or by any means, without the prior permission in writing from the publisher, nor be otherwise circulated in any form of binding or cover other than that in which it is published and without a similar condition including this condition being imposed on the subsequent purchaser.

First published in Great Britain in 2015 by The Amethyst Angel

Copyright © 2015 by Michelle Gordon

Cover Design by madappledesigns

Copyright © The Amethyst Angel

ISBN: 978-1517766313

The moral right of the author has been asserted.

All characters and events in this publication, other than those clearly in the public domain are fictitious, and any resemblance to real persons, living or dead, is purely coincidental.

First Edition

Gratitude

As always, there are so many people to thank for helping me to create this book, it really isn't something I do all by myself! So, here goes:

First of all, I would like to express my gratitude for my sister, Liz Gordon, who has not only created all of the amazing covers for the Earth Angel Series and the Visionary Collection, but she has also supported me in many other ways, without which, much of what I have achieved would not be possible. She puts up with my short deadlines, last-minute requests and general annoying behaviour, all with good humour and love. I would like to gift 50% ownership of this book to my amazing Starperson sister, as a token of my gratitude for all she has done for me.

Lizzie, you really are out of this world, love you lots. xxx

Big thank you to my beta readers and editors, Sally Byrne and Liz Lockwood, you both love and support me and keep me sane, as well as help to make the book the best it can be, and I am so thankful to you both for that!

Much love to my Camp Nanowrimo buddies, Rachael Barnwell & Tiffany Hathorn, for joining me in the writing madness in July, you both made the camping experience far more fun. I enjoyed the s'mores!

A gigantic thank you to all of my readers, without your reviews, feedback and support, I would feel quite lonely! Philip James, Saeed Jabbari, Malinda Rose, Andrew Embling, Cyndi Sabido, Sian Williams, Harri Emma, Dawn Norman, Willow Jordan, Annette Ecuyere, Emily Jarvis, Helen Roberts, Rachel Robinson, Andrea Degan, Rosa Ivy, Robyn Peters, Annemarie Harris, Debbie Freeman, Ana Dueñas León, Alexandra Laura Payne, Noelia Rodriguez, Shelley Brookdale, Jill Dimos, Nadina Lee, Xander,

Jacqueline Wigglesworth, Nicky Lee, Cheryl Cave, Tadhg Jonathan Gardner, Wenda Prior, and Valerie Abl.

And of course, love, hugs and gratitude to my wonderful friends and family who put up with my craziness and cheer me on – Jon Fellows, Sally Byrne, Liz Lockwood, Helen Gordon, Niki, Chip Jenkins, Meg Kate, Lucja Fratczak-Kay, Sarah Vine, Miranda Adams, Louise Brister and Hannah Jones.

This book is dedicated to Liz Gordon.
For being the best alien sister an old soul could ask for.

Chapter One

"Hey, miss, are you okay?"

Helen blinked and forced herself to concentrate on the face peering at her. She processed the words spoken then slowly nodded, though really she wanted to shake her head. The stranger seemed to be appeased with her false nod and left her to drift in the sea of bodies that swarmed past her, all busy going somewhere. She was going nowhere. She was stuck, rooted to the spot.

After being bumped into a few more times, she managed to move herself a few steps sideways, and collapse onto a park bench outside one of the shops. She watched the people going by with their shopping bags, laughing, having fun, and she couldn't believe that she was a human being too, just like them. And that fun was something she could have.

It didn't seem like a possibility right in that moment.

Her phone buzzed in her pocket. It took her a few moments to register the sound and then pull it out and press the green button.

"Helen, where are you?" A tear escaped from her eye at the sound of her friend's voice. She was unable to respond immediately.

"Helen? Are you okay? He didn't hurt you did he? What happened? Wherever you are, I'll come to you."

"I'm okay," Helen managed to whisper. "He didn't hurt me. He just wouldn't leave. So I did. I've left him. Now I don't know what to do."

"You'll come to mine. Tell me where you are and I'll come and get you."

"I haven't got anything with me," Helen said.

"That doesn't matter, I have everything you might need, and anything else, we can get. Now where are you?"

Helen told Maggie where she was, then she hung up. Though she wanted to just curl up, go to sleep and not wake up, she knew that Maggie would help her get back on track.

Less than ten minutes later, her phone buzzed in her hand. She answered it, then followed Maggie's instructions to find where she was parked.

When she spotted the old, dented red Fiat, the tears started up again. She opened the passenger door and slid inside. She looked across at Maggie, who reached over and pulled her into a brief hug before pulling away from the curb.

They didn't speak the whole way to Maggie's home, and Helen was glad of the quiet. Her life and her mind had been so chaotic recently, it was a relief to not have to fill the silence.

Once inside the house with a shot of whiskey in front of her, Helen spoke.

"I didn't have any other choice. He didn't understand that I couldn't live like that anymore. I love him, but I would rather not be here than live another day in the same way."

"Oh, sweetheart," Maggie said, wrapping her arms around her and holding her tight. "You did the right thing. It's time to put your own wellbeing first. I can see you've lost your sparkle."

Tears streamed down Helen's face and soaked into Maggie's top. "I'm just so tired of fighting, Maggie. I don't want to fight anymore."

"The spare room is ready. Drink up, get in the shower, get into the PJs I've set out, then get into bed and do not even think about leaving it until you've had a proper rest."

Helen nodded and Maggie released her so she could drink her whiskey. She winced at the burning sensation as she slugged it down, but it did warm her up. She followed Maggie's instructions to a T and half an hour later, was tucked up under the covers.

Despite the heavy sadness in her heart, and the tiredness and pain she had endured, as she drifted off to sleep, there was a part of her that was relieved. It was over. It was time for a new chapter.

One that didn't involve him.

* * *

"Where do people think it goes when they drop litter? Do they have no respect for the sea life or the other people on the beach?" Sherrie asked her friend Sylvie as she picked up yet another beer can from the white sand.

Sylvie sighed. "I don't know, maybe they think the litter faeries come and sort it out." She raised an eyebrow at her friend and Sherrie giggled and felt some of the tension from her frustration lift from her shoulders. She got so angry about people dropping litter on the beach, as it ended up in the ocean and killed sea life. She felt very strongly about protecting the life that inhabited the waters. She loved swimming in the sea, and the idea of it being lifeless made her feel utter despair.

"Besides, it's your purpose, isn't it? You're here on this planet to educate humans about their habits, which are destroying the oceans. So if none of them littered, what would you have left to do?"

Sherrie shook her head. "I somehow can't imagine a world where there are no idiots destroying the planet."

Sylvie bent down to pick up several food packets and her nose wrinkled in disgust as she picked up a soiled nappy and put it in her trash bag. "But if you can't imagine it, how can we create it?"

Sherrie closed her eyes and screwed up her face. She was just so tired of taking a few steps forward, only to be pushed even further back. It was like fighting the tide, futile. She plopped down on the sand, and her gaze wandered around her. All she could see was the trash. She couldn't see the beauty of the scene, she just saw the ugliness left behind by other people.

Sylvie sat next to her, and pulled off her rubber gloves. "Sherr, what's going on? You usually have so much energy for our sessions, but it feels like you're just not here. Is everything okay with you and Jim?"

Sherrie sighed. "Not really. We just seem to be fighting all the time. He doesn't understand that I need to do this, that I need to do everything I can to clean up the beaches and the ocean. And to bring people's awareness to the consequences of their thoughtlessness. He just wants me to work in a normal job and make some money so we're not struggling to pay the bills every month."

Sylvie nodded, but said nothing. She waited patiently for Sherrie to continue.

"And I can see his point, after all, it's like fighting a losing battle, I mean, we clean this beach every week. And we fill several trash bags every week. And no matter how many events I hold, how many talks I do, people aren't changing their habits, their lifestyles. It just all feels so pointless." She turned to Sylvie, and shook her head. "You say it's my purpose on this planet to do this work, but if it make no difference, why should I bother?"

Sylvie considered her words for a while before replying. Sherrie knew that she wasn't particularly keen on Jim, so she was probably trying to find something kind to say, even though she wanted to bitch about him.

"Struggling with finances is always going to be a relationship killer," Sylvie said. "Look at me and Robbie. We argued nonstop about money, and we just couldn't do it anymore. Our priorities and values were just too different for us to be able to work things out together. I miss the good stuff about being with him, but I know that the bad times far outweighed the good. And now we're apart, we've both really sorted ourselves out." Sylvie shrugged. "I may not be rich, but

I manage on my wage at the library."

Sherrie nodded. She and Jim did have very different views on finances, it was true.

"I personally think that you are so lucky to know what your purpose is, what you are passionate about. Because I don't know what mine is. I don't know what I'm here for. I just know that I love to read, and that my job gives me access to a lot of free books. Other than that, I'm just living, just being here."

Sherrie smiled at her friend. "I'm very glad you're here. And you do amazing things all the time. You do so much for me, and for your other friends. Maybe just loving people is your mission."

Sylvie smiled back. "That's a pretty cool mission. I can do that."

Feeling a little less burdened, Sherrie jumped to her feet then held out a gloved hand to her friend. "Shall we get this beach sparkling again?"

Sylvie took her hand and saluted her. "Yes, ma'am. Let's do it!"

Sherrie giggled and continued to pick up the trash. She paused for a moment as the sun burst through the clouds, shining down on them. She lifted her face to the light, and smiled. Yes, it was her purpose to be here, doing this. Even if it felt like a losing battle, it was one that she had to continue.

She knew there was a reason for it all. She just hoped that one day she would know what the reason was.

*　　*　　*

"Why do you think so many people are breaking up with their partners at the moment?"

Violet tilted her head to one side, considering the question asked by one of her workshop participants. "Does it seem like a lot of relationships are breaking up?" she asked. She didn't appear surprised to see most of the heads in the room nodding.

After all, it was a workshop on finding your Twin Flame.

"I have very few friends in stable relationships," Julie offered, surprising herself by speaking up. She normally kept to herself during these things, but she was curious too.

"I think we're experiencing a dramatic shift in consciousness at the moment," Violet said. "And one of the side-effects of this is that we can no longer tolerate situations that aren't good for us. If we're in relationships that are toxic in any way, we're finding ways to get out of those situations. We're becoming more aware and Awake, and we're realising that it's impossible for us to be here and live lives full of passion and purpose if we're around someone who drains us of our energy."

Julie nodded. She could relate to that. Whereas she had put up with all of her husband's foibles before, in the last couple of years, they seemed to be magnified to the point where she could no longer see his light. She could no longer remember why she loved him. Which was why she was planning to leave. She just hadn't worked out how to do that when she had three children and would have to support them and herself. He'd been the breadwinner for the last ten years, while she had been a stay-at-home mum and housewife.

He had no idea where she was at that moment, he thought she was visiting a friend, and having some rare time to herself. But she had seen the Twin Flame workshop advertised in a spiritual magazine and she just knew that she had to attend it. It felt a little like cheating, attending a workshop that was aimed at helping people to meet a partner, when she had a husband and children waiting for her at home.

But she had to make some changes in her life. She felt like every day, a little more of her died. She was desperate to start living her true purpose in this lifetime, and she knew that it just wouldn't be possible to do that within her current relationship.

Julie brought her attention back to the room, and focussed on what Violet was saying. She hadn't read her book yet, but had bought a copy earlier in the day, and planned to read it that evening. With the kids demanding all of her attention she couldn't even remember the last time she had read anything longer than a blog post or a magazine article.

"I also believe that the Twin Flames have been activated in the last couple of years, which means that suddenly, people are aware that they have a Flame out there somewhere, who is their true soulmate, the one that they can have the most amazing relationship with. And this has caused people to get irritated with their current partners, and to begin moving away from them. Before that, people were content to remain in a relationship until death, because their love was very much on a human level."

Julie raised her hand again. "By that, do you mean on a superficial level?"

Violet frowned and shook her head. "No, human love is very real and deep and beautiful, but it is very much three dimensional. The Twin Flame love is something that permeates so many more levels and dimensions and is all encompassing."

"That sounds like it would distract you from your purpose, if it's that intense," Julie said, surprising herself again by continuing to speak up. It was a fairly small group, but she still didn't like to speak in public if she could avoid it.

Violet smiled at her. "You're right. It is very distracting, and my Flame and I find that we get very little done when we're around each other all the time, which is why it is so important to give each other space. I think that holds true for any relationship, but in order to maintain a Twin Flame connection, it is even more so, because of the intensity. But it can be difficult to do. To be away from your Flame, even if you are still together in a relationship, can feel terrible. It takes a lot of getting used to. I have had to get used to it, with all the travelling I have done, running these workshops and doing book signings and talks around the country. I count down the days until I see him again, but the time away also strengthens our bond, and knowing that he loves me so deeply helps me to carry out my mission."

Julie felt tears gathering in her eyes, and she nodded. What Violet was describing was how she wanted to feel in a relationship. She wanted a secure, solid foundation, but also the freedom to fly and fulfil her purpose.

"You said that the Twin Flames were being activated, so does that mean that people are more likely to find their Flame now? Are they energetically drawn to one another?"

Violet nodded to the lady who'd asked the question. "Yes, I believe so. When you hear some of the many stories of how people come to meet their Flames, they are quite incredible. They are often not the typical 'boy meets girl' scenario."

"What do you mean by that?" the lady asked.

Julie listened with interest as Violet talked about the different ways that Flames had come to meet, including sea rescues, dog attacks and caving incidents.

"Does that mean that if you meet someone in a calm and ordered way they're not likely to be your Twin Flame?" another lady asked.

Everyone in the room laughed, and Violet shook her head. "I really hope not. I don't think that the circumstances of the meeting need to be dramatic, but it does seem that in the intensity of the moment, it is easier to recognise your Flame. Which takes us into the next topic of today's workshop – how to recognise your Twin Flame."

Julie took copious notes for the rest of the afternoon, trying to keep up with the information that Violet was giving them. By the end of the day, she felt exhausted, but exhilarated at the same time. She knew that she wanted to experience the Twin Flame connection, and that somehow, finding her Flame would help her to find her true mission and purpose.

As she walked back to the hotel later, she was looking forward to having a long, hot bath and reading Violet's book. She couldn't remember the last time she'd had the luxury of reading in the bathtub, it used to be her favourite way to relax.

Glass of wine to hand, soft music playing in the background; Julie sank into the bubbles, opened the book to the first page, and lost herself in a world of Faeries and Angels.

Chapter Two

"Are you kidding me? What are you braking for? Get off the road if you can't drive!"

Tadhg tried to calm himself, but his road rage was about to rip out of control. He just didn't have the patience to be stuck behind someone who braked every time a car came in the opposite direction.

"They're on the other side of the road, you idiot!" he screamed at the car in front. "They're not going to hit you!"

His rage boiled hotter and hotter, and he couldn't bear it another second. Without bothering to indicate, he pulled out and overtook the car, but he hadn't calculated the amount of time it would take to pass them, and found himself heading into a blind bend on the wrong side of the road. By the time he registered the car heading toward him, he already knew it was too late to take any action to prevent the collision.

The force of the impact threw him forward, and because he'd been in such a hurry to get to the interview, he hadn't bothered putting on his seatbelt, which he sorely regretted when his head struck the windscreen and the pain of the glass breaking on his crown rippled through his whole body.

He blacked out then, and was surprised to find himself standing in a white mist.

"Greetings, Tartan. I daresay that your impatience has brought you back here again."

Tadhg blinked at the white-haired man, his memories of

his previous life rushing back to him. "Gold," he said, remembering the Elder's name. "What do you mean, again?"

Gold smiled. "During this short lifetime, you have ended up here in these mists, being asked the Ultimate Question, five times now. And every time, it was your anger and impatience that caused the crossing."

"Crossing? Shit, I'm dead." Tadhg looked around him, and marvelled at how the pain in his body had disappeared completely. He looked down at his red robes, and wished that he hadn't had to leave his job at the Earth Angel Training Academy. At least he'd been respected then. He'd had authority, and was looked up to. On Earth, he'd worked in crappy minimum wage jobs where he was treated like dirt. It was no wonder he had so much anger and impatience inside him.

"Why do I keep choosing to go back?" he asked. "I could stay here, couldn't I?"

"Of course you could. You know that. We would welcome you as a guide, or you could go home to the stars."

Tadhg frowned. It was tempting, staying here. Earth sucked as much as he always taught his students that it did. Humans were evil, arrogant, stupid creatures. And it was killing him to have to spend so much time around them. "You didn't answer my question, why do I keep choosing to go back?"

"I don't know," Gold said. "Why do you?"

Tadhg had to stop himself from swearing at the old man, he could be downright infuriating at times. He scanned the memories available to him, and he came upon a conversation he'd had with his Guardian Angel just before entering his new life on Earth.

"She promised I would meet my Twin Flame," he said out loud without thinking about it. "That's why I keep returning, because I've yet to meet her." He shook his head and looked at Gold. "I just don't see how it's possible. Every human I have ever met has been a life-sucking, arrogant, miserable creature.

And if my Flame is the same way, then quite frankly, I'd rather stay here and remain by myself."

Gold tilted his head and considered this. "Have you ever heard of the idea that the people and situations around you are simply mirrors of your internal self?"

Tadhg raised his eyebrows. "Are you saying that I'm a life-sucking miserable creature?"

"An arrogant one, yes," Gold agreed.

Tadhg's mouth dropped open. "That's a bit harsh isn't it?"

"Remember, I am just a mirror."

"So now you're saying I'm harsh too."

"Tartan, I believe there is so much good in you, but you have been hiding it away for so long, you have forgotten it exists."

Tadhg frowned. "I'm just me. This is just the way I am. I cannot change it, I have been this way for hundreds of lifetimes as a human. In the same way that Corduroy was obsessed with death, guns and violence, and Cotton was incredibly patient," he said, referring to his colleagues at the Academy. "It's just who we have developed into being over time."

Gold sighed. "When will you finally grasp the concept that time is irrelevant, that how long you have been a certain way is irrelevant? The only thing that is relevant is whether you are motivated enough to first of all decide to change, and then to make those changes happen."

Tadhg snorted. "You're even crazier than I thought. There are some things that you just can't change. Do you honestly think that I can go back, wake up from this accident and suddenly start acting like Pollyanna on crack? Come, on, Gold. That's just crazy."

Gold shrugged. "If you say so. Don't forget though, that this is a second take. That the life you are living now, you have already lived. And so if you wish to meet the same fate as you previously did, you are heading in exactly the right direction. I just thought you might like to try something different this time. Just for fun."

Tadhg felt himself shudder at the word fun, but he considered what Gold had said. He became aware then, of the first time he'd lived this life, and how he'd ended up miserable and alone at the end of the world. When he'd arrived back on the other side, he'd been relieved to be back where he felt at home. He'd nearly decided not to go back for the second take, because why would he want to experience that again?

Oh yes, because he hadn't met his Twin Flame in that life, and he hoped that he would this time round.

"Was she lying to me?"

Gold frowned. "Was who lying to you?"

"My Guardian Angel. She said I would meet my Flame. But I didn't the first time around. And I haven't met her yet this time either. So maybe she was just lying to me to get me to go to earth to experience the human misery for the thousand and four hundredth time."

"Our time is nearly up, you are about to be resuscitated for the final time. Do you wish to stay? Or will you return?"

Tadhg was annoyed that Gold evaded his question yet again. "What if nothing changes?"

"It only will if you do."

Tadhg sighed. "Fine. I'll go back."

Gold smiled at his tone. "Good luck, Tartan. May you be blessed and loved."

"Yeah, right, whatever," Tadhg muttered, as he stomped back into the mists, away from the Elder.

The white fog rose up to meet him and suddenly he was jolted forward and a shock slammed through his chest making him gasp. When he opened his eyes he made eye contact with a woman leaning over him.

"He's back, we've got him back."

As the doctors and nurses rushed around him, Tadhg relaxed back into the bed, and closed his eyes. A few moments later, he became aware of his body and the shock of pain from his head crashed down on him, making him gasp before he slipped into oblivion.

* * *

"Oh, come on, have a drink, everyone else is."

Josh sighed. Ever since he'd turned seventeen, the pressure to drink and go out clubbing had become crazy. At what point would his friends get it that he really wasn't interested? He shook his head and walked out of the kitchen, and without thinking it through, he picked up his jacket from the hallway, opened the front door and stepped outside into the cool night air. Once the door was closed behind him and the music faded a little, he looked up at the stars and made the decision not to try to fit in with his peers any longer.

A smile on his face, he slung his jacket over his shoulder and walked down the path, leaving the house party behind him. It was only eleven o'clock, and he knew that his mum would be worrying about where he was. But he wasn't quite ready to go home yet.

He found himself walking to the castle grounds, which was on the way home. The ruin shone in the moonlight, and he leaned his back against the stone wall, connecting with the energy of the stones, which had stood for several hundred years. He felt the pain of all the atrocities the stone had witnessed, and the guilt the stone felt for not being able to stop it.

A tear ran down his cheek. He knew that feeling of futility. He had felt it too, many times. He no longer watched the news for it made him feel so helpless, unable to help those who were suffering. He preferred to send prayers out every day, to any and all who needed them.

He was not a typical seventeen-year-old by any means. He had been 'normal' once. But that felt like a weird dream now. He breathed in deeply and shook his head. He didn't want to think about that time. Because it would lead to thinking about what had caused his shift in consciousness, and it still felt too raw to delve into.

He thanked the stone for sharing its energy with him, then he straightened up, and set off home.

When Josh approached his house and saw that the lounge lights were still on, he sighed. He didn't think his mum would ever stop worrying about him.

He put his key in the lock and turned it, quietly opening the front door. He went into the lounge and kissed his mother on the forehead. "I'm home, Mum," he said quietly, making her stir from her light sleep. "Go to bed."

She opened her eyes and looked relieved to see him. She nodded and got up slowly, stretching as she did so. She smiled sleepily at him as she passed him and went upstairs. He switched off the lamp, then went to the kitchen to find something to eat.

Once safely in his bedroom with a cheese sandwich, Josh sat on his bed and pulled out the book he was currently reading. It was different to any other book he'd read, and it was stretching him a little, but he knew that it contained things that he needed to remember.

He bit into his sandwich and flipped to the page he had bookmarked. He continued to read about the Starpeople with interest, ignoring the late hour and the fact that he had college in the morning.

Chapter Three

"Excuse me?"

Julie was shaking a little bit as she tried to get Violet's attention. She had spotted her in the café attached to the hotel, and decided to bite the bullet and speak to her. She clutched her copy of *The Earth Angel Training Academy*, now a little damp and wrinkled from having been read almost entirely in the bath the previous evening.

She moved a little closer to the Old Soul who was reading something on her laptop, and she cleared her throat and tried again. "Excuse me, Violet?"

At the sound of her name, Violet looked up and registered that she was standing there. She looked at the book in Julie's hand and then smiled.

"You were in the workshop yesterday," she said, closing her laptop and putting it down on the coffee table. "How are you today, Earth Angel?"

Julie smiled nervously, and sat down opposite her, feeling a little starstruck. "I'm good, thank you. I'm really sorry to bother you, if you're busy, I can go."

Violet shook her head. "Don't be silly, I was just catching up on some emails, they can wait. You look as though you have something you need to talk about."

Julie nodded. "Yes, I enjoyed the workshop yesterday, and I bought your book, and I read it all last night."

Violet's eyes widened. "You didn't get much sleep then?"

Julie laughed. "No, not much. But I had to finish it to find out what happened in the end. You're Velvet, aren't you?"

Violet smiled. "Yes, the character is based on myself, and the book is based on visions I've had, memories that I have accessed from past lives. Did you resonate with the story?"

Without meaning to, Julie started to cry. She nodded, and Violet leaned forward to touch her hand. "I was there," Julie whispered. "I was the Professor of Patience."

Violet's eyes widened and searched hers. Tears formed in the Old Soul's eyes and she gripped her hands.

"Cotton?" she said. "Is it really you?"

Julie nodded. She knew it so clearly. Reading Violet's book had been like going home, going back to where she belonged.

Violet's tears fell, and she smiled. "My dear Old Soul, it is so good to see you again." She shook her head. "I have so far only reconnected with Athena, I have not yet met the incarnations of the other professors."

Julie smiled. "How is Athena? All of my life, I have felt as though I deeply missed something, but could not work out what it was. Reading your book made me realise that it was the Academy, and all the amazing souls who worked there. Goddess, I miss you all." More tears fell, and Julie dug in her pocket for a tissue to wipe them away.

"I miss the Academy too, but I know that it's important to be here. Didn't you say yesterday that you have three children? I bet they are Crystal and Indigo Children, aren't they?"

Julie thought about her beautiful sons and daughter and then nodded. "Yes, I think they might well be."

"Then you have done an amazing thing, bringing beautiful Golden Age Children into the world. It's fine to miss the Other Side, but we will all go home again one day, so we may as well make the most of what we have here, now."

Julie nodded. "I understand that, and I do think that I have more patience than most," she said wryly. Both she and Violet laughed. "But I have recently been feeling such a strong pull to live my passion, my purpose. And though I'm not certain exactly what my purpose is yet, I am certain I cannot live it while I'm with my husband. It feels like his energy is so dense and dark, he just pulls me backwards every time I feel like I'm finally moving forward."

Violet nodded. "I can certainly relate to that. It's so important for us to surround ourselves with people that lift us up, that are vibrating in the same way. When someone is vibrating at a lower level, it can stop us from living our purpose."

"What did you do, when you were in the same situation?"

Violet sighed. "I cut them out of my life. I wish I could say that I lifted them into the light with me, but at the time, I honestly didn't have the energy to be able to do so. I think that now, I would have the energy to do that, but I wouldn't even know how to begin reaching out to them. I just have to hope that we were in each other's lives for that short period of time for a reason, and that one day, we will meet again, on the same level, and be friends."

Julie nodded. "That's how I feel about my husband. I love him, I want the best for him, but I don't feel like we're the best for each other right now, I feel like I'm stuck, and no matter how much patience I have, I'm slowly withering away."

"We can't have that," Violet said. "What can I do to help?"

Julie sighed. "I appreciate the offer, but I think this is something I have to figure out for myself. I haven't ever really stood on my own two feet, I was content to let him take care of everything. But it's time to change that. I need to be my own person, and I need to show my children that I can take care of them myself, and that they can be independent too."

"How old are they?"

"Charlotte is ten, Daniel is eight and Jerry is just six."

Violet smiled. "I'm sure that they know what a beautiful soul you are. And they will adjust to the changes that you make. The Children of the Golden Age are particularly open to new things."

Julie nodded slowly. "I just find it overwhelming, when I think of everything I would need to make happen to be able to separate from my husband. And I really don't think he's going to take it very well, either."

"Just remember to ask the Angels to help you," Violet said. "They're around you, all the time, just waiting for you to ask for their assistance. And my offer still stands, if there is anything at all I can do to help, then please ask. You could come and stay with Greg and I at the Retreat for a bit if you need somewhere to stay."

Julie smiled. "Thank you, I can't believe that you're offering that to someone you barely even know, it's amazing."

Violet stood and Julie followed suit. The two Old Souls embraced and Violet whispered into her ear. "You are one of my closest friends, one of my bravest warriors here on Earth. I wish to assist you in any way I can, to live your purpose."

Tears streamed down Julie's cheeks, and she nodded into Violet's soft shoulder. "Thank you," she whispered back. "Thank you, Velvet. I have missed you."

"I've missed you too, Cotton. I've missed you too."

* * *

After three days in Maggie's care, Helen was beginning to feel more like her old self. She hadn't realised just how sleep deprived she had become. She slept for a full eighteen hours to begin with, and then for ten hours the following nights. Things were already looking a lot clearer.

As she tucked into the delicious vegetarian meal that Maggie had made her, she was aware of her friend watching her closely. She smiled at her. "You okay?"

Maggie nodded. "I'm fine. How are you? Your energy seems a lot lighter now, but I get the feeling that there is something that needs clearing yet."

Helen frowned. She felt a lot better than she had a few days previously, after leaving her home and her partner for the last time. She supposed that she did have a little bit of fear of where to go from here. After all, she didn't have any savings to live on, and her job paid her a paltry wage. She couldn't rely on her friend taking care of her for too long, it wasn't fair.

She swallowed another mouthful of carrots and nodded slowly. "I'm feeling a little bit at a loss of what do to next. I don't want to rely on you too much, and I'm absolutely determined not to go back, but where do I go? What do I do?"

Maggie's gaze shifted a little, and she stared at something unseen over Helen's left shoulder. Helen's heartbeat jumped a little, as she knew that it meant Maggie was getting visions of what might come to pass. Was she ready to hear what her future might hold?

When her friend frowned her heart dropped into her feet, she really didn't feel ready to hear what she had to say. But before she could protest, Maggie's gaze refocussed and met hers.

"Have you ever done any travelling?"

Helen frowned this time, setting her fork down. As a young child, she had dreamed of travelling the world, of visiting as many countries as possible. She wanted to learn languages, experience different cultures, and eat local delicacies. But those dreams had dissipated in the sludge of her daily reality.

"No. I haven't ever left the UK. I don't even have a passport." She shrugged. "I never saw the point in having one, when I wasn't going anywhere."

"Get one now," her friend said. "Because I can see that England is no longer where you need to be. I will help you if money is an issue. It's time to release all excuses and start living your purpose on this planet."

Helen's eyes widened. "What did you See?"

Maggie smiled. "I Saw that you are going to make a huge difference. And that you are going to change the world, along with the other Earth Angels."

Tears began to roll down Helen's cheeks. She had given

up on the idea that she could possibly make any difference in this lifetime. She didn't feel as though she had much to offer others. But perhaps she was wrong. Perhaps there was enough time to change that.

"There's always enough time," Maggie said softly, as though reading her thoughts. "Just believe, it will happen."

Helen nodded and picked her fork back up, her appetite returning suddenly. Her mind was already whizzing ahead, thinking of what she would need to sort out in order to get her first passport.

"It's time to fly, my Faerie friend," Maggie said with a grin. "It's most definitely time to fly."

Chapter Four

Sherrie scowled at her computer screen as she read yet another article about the amount of trash that was washing up on the shores of beaches all around the world. She shared it on her Facebook page, then she opened up another one, this time about sharks who were having their fins cut off to make soup, and then were tossed back into the ocean alive, so they could die on the ocean floor. She was almost shaking with anger, while her heart was breaking into a thousand pieces.

How was it possible that the world could be so damned cruel? That these humans could even sleep at night after committing such atrocities? Did they not understand that they were destroying the oceans? Destroying the planet? Wrecking the equilibrium of life on Earth?

She shared the post about the sharks, even though the images turned her stomach. She signed the petition to stop shark hunting, and then she got up to make herself a drink. It took her a few minutes to calm herself down again, and to slow her heart rate. She couldn't help getting so emotionally involved. She just wished there was more she could do.

Cleaning up her local beach, educating local people and children and bringing awareness to the issues through social media just didn't seem like enough. She wanted to make a real difference, not just a superficial one. Otherwise, why was she here?

As she sipped her iced tea, her eye settled on a framed

photograph of herself on the beach, wearing her favourite mermaid tail. Her smile was radiant and the sun was glistening in her red hair.

She wished she could go back to those carefree days. Slipping on a mermaid tail and going to the pool or to the beach was her favourite past-time, but after a certain point, it just felt like she was burying her head in the sand and ignoring the real issues that existed. So she put the tails away, and promised herself not to get them back out until the world was a better place, and that having fun was allowed again.

It didn't look like that would actually happen in her lifetime.

Sherrie sat back down at her laptop, and was partway through watching a video of a whale being freed from a fishing net when a new email notification pinged on her phone.

She pressed the button and opened the email, still half watching the video. A few words in the email caught her eye and she stopped the video, giving the message her full attention. By the time she'd finished reading it, her mouth was wide open in surprise.

It was from a charity that focussed on saving sea life. They had seen her photos and videos online of her mermaid days, and wanted her to become the voice and face of the charity. They wanted her to work with them to not only raise awareness of the plight of the sea life that was dying out thanks to human pollution and cruelty, but also be actively involved in their rescue missions.

Her heart started beating faster, only this time in excitement. It was the perfect opportunity. She could be her mermaid self, and also do something real, something practical to help the animals that she loved so much.

But what about Jim? Taking their offer would mean travelling. A lot of it. And she wasn't sure he would be okay with that.

She heard the front door open and close, and she exited her emails on her phone. She figured she would find out. She logged off of Facebook and put the computer in hibernation mode.

"Hey, sweetie," she called out, going to greet him. "How was work?"

The look on Jim's face told her everything she needed to know, and for a while, Sherrie put her amazing opportunity to the back of her mind, and busied herself with making food for her husband; letting him rant and rave about his idiot colleagues while she did so. She wished he could take a job that he actually enjoyed, but she knew that if she made a suggestion to that effect, he would go into a rant about how he had to pay the bills and rent, and he didn't have the luxury of doing what he was passionate about.

Which was all true, but at the same time, Sherrie didn't want to live like that.

"Jim, I had an email today," she said, once they were sat opposite each other at the table out on the deck of their tiny apartment.

"Big deal, I had a hundred emails today, all from total assholes too," Jim retorted.

Sherrie took a deep breath, ignored his negativity and tried again. "It was from Fishy Friends. They want me to work for them, helping them to raise awareness of problems in the ocean. But not only raise awareness, they want me to help them to rescue the animals too."

Jim raised an eyebrow and put his fork down. "Why am I getting the feeling that I'm not going to like what you have to say next?"

Sherrie looked down at her plate. "It means a lot of travel, a lot of time away from home. But it's what I really want to do, it's what I love." She looked up and called on the elements for strength. "And I'm going to say yes. It's an amazing opportunity, and I really don't want to miss it."

Jim pushed his chair back in disgust. "Well why even bother mentioning it to me? Why not just pack your bags and leave a note if you've already decided? So much for having discussions about big things."

He stalked off, slamming the sliding glass door back and heading for the kitchen, where she knew he would be helping himself to another beer.

Despite his reaction, Sherrie felt a wave of excitement wash over her as she considered the proposal. Her weariness had lifted a little, and she knew that this was her chance to make a real difference. She slowly finished her dinner, but Jim didn't re-join her. When she cleared the table and went inside, she found him hunched over his laptop, the glow of the screen lighting the frown on his face.

She took everything to the kitchen and cleaned up, then she headed to their bedroom, taking her phone with her. She opened the email again and re-read it, then she hit reply, and started to write her acceptance email.

She couldn't wait to tell Sylvie all about her upcoming adventure.

* * *

The first thing Tadhg became aware of, was a female voice incorrectly pronouncing his name. He could feel the irritation rising up within him, as she repeated it softly over and over. Finally, he couldn't bear it any longer, and without even opening his eyes, he snapped, "It's Tadhg, okay? Like the beginning of tiger. Stop saying it wrong."

There was a stifled giggle and the female voice spoke again. "I think he's back with us."

He sighed and opened one eye, squinting at the owner of the voice. A familiar pair of eyes stared back. It was the face he'd woken up to directly after the accident.

Accident. He did a quick survey of his body, wiggling his fingers and moving his legs, but when he tried to move his left leg, found that he couldn't.

He tried to look down but could only see the white sheets that were covering him. "Why can't I move my leg?" he asked, not caring that he sounded rude.

The nurse sighed, looking like she wished she didn't have to answer his question. "I'm afraid your leg was too badly injured in the accident to save. It's been amputated just above the knee."

Tadhg stared at the nurse in horror. "I'm sorry, it sounded like you just said they chopped my leg off."

"Yes, I'm afraid so." She fiddled with his IV and wrote some notes on a clipboard, avoiding his gaze. He blinked, terrified that he would start crying. He never cried. The last time he'd felt so much as even a slight moistening of his eyes was when he'd learnt that his dad had died in an accident twenty years previously.

"Please leave me alone," he barked at the nurse, who complied with his request, looking like she was about to cry herself.

Unable to fully believe her words, he grabbed the sheets and pulled them to one side, then propped himself up on his elbow, ignoring the throbbing in his skull, and stared down at what was left of his left leg. He tried to run the accident through his mind, but all he could remember was the impact of his head shattering the windscreen. How had his leg become injured? It didn't make any sense.

"Doctor!" he yelled. "Nurse!"

Another nurse came into the room moments later, looking a little alarmed. "What's wrong, do you need more painkillers?" she went over to his IV and adjusted it, then she gave him the buzzer. "If you need us, just press this."

"Why was my leg mangled? I don't understand. I went through the windscreen, but I blacked out after that. Do you know what happened?"

The nurse checked his notes. "It appears that after you were thrown clear of your car through the windscreen, another car then accidentally drove over your leg as you lay on the road."

Tadhg's eyes widened. "Are you serious? What? They

couldn't see I was lying there? Were they blind?"

"No offence, sir, but it also says that you were the one who caused the accident by illegally overtaking another vehicle on a bend. If I were you, I would be thanking the Lord that I'm alive, praying that none of the other injured parties sues me, and hoping that I don't get charged for dangerous driving."

Tadhg blinked. Her tone irritated him. Grateful for losing his leg? As if! "Yes well, I'm not you. Surely they could have done more to save my leg. I mean really, with today's technology? It's ridiculous."

The nurse sighed and put his notes back. "Press the buzzer if you need more medication. I need to go and check on the other victims of the accident."

"Fine," Tadhg said. She sounded like she was annoyed at having to waste her precious time on caring for him. What a cow.

He shifted about, trying to get comfortable, and he pulled the sheets back over his legs, unable to look at them anymore. He spotted a glass of water on the bedside table and took a sip. His stomach growled and he wondered how long it would be until they fed him. They hadn't even asked him if he wanted to contact anyone, how inconsiderate could you get? He'd nearly died! And he'd lost his leg. His anger and rage began to stir, and he ignored the fact that they probably hadn't asked, because they knew that he had no one to call.

Chapter Five

"Josh! You're going to be late for college. Get up!"
Josh blinked sleepily, the morning sunlight was streaming through his window. He smiled at the warmth of it on his face.
"What are you smiling for?" his mum asked. "If you think I'm taking you in, you're sadly mistaken. Now get up."
Josh nodded, and hauled himself out of bed. He'd been up until the early hours again, devouring another spiritual book. He just couldn't get enough information it seemed. He had gone through all of the texts in the local library and was now scouring second-hand bookshops and charity shops, hungry for more. He threw some clothes on, picked up his bag, still packed from the previous day, and left his room. His mum handed him a banana and a foil-wrapped sandwich – his usual cheese salad no doubt – then he headed out the door to college. By the time he got the bus and arrived in the art department, he was thirty-five minutes late.
He caught the attention of his tutor, who rolled her eyes and marked down in the register that he was present. She was used to the tardiness of her art students, and by now, she had given up on penalising them for it. She knew that they always made up for the lost time anyway.
Josh dumped his bag on the floor next to his desk, and glanced at the sheet of paper that lay waiting for him. It seemed that they had to paint a piece entitled 'Dream'. It was quite a vague guideline, and Josh was intrigued. The project

briefs were usually much more detailed than that. He glanced around the room and saw wildly varying works of art in progress being created by his peers. Shrugging to himself, he got his art materials out of the drawer and picked out a fresh canvas from his stocks. Rather than follow his classmates' example, Josh decided to make his piece more 3D and re-create a dream he'd had the previous night, of being inside a cave of all different crystals. He wanted to make it look like the crystals were coming out of the canvas. He set to work, doing a pencil drawing first, then creating crystal-like sculptures out of wire and air-dry clay. By lunchtime, he had finished the 3D part, and decided to take it outside with him into the sunshine to make it dry faster so he could finish it that afternoon.

He kept to himself during lunch, preferring to sit in a sunny spot on the grass and read more his latest book than to socialise with the others.

"Good book?"

Josh looked up, squinting into the sunlight at the figure casting a shadow over him. He smiled when he recognised Maisy.

"Yes, I can't seem to stop reading it," Josh replied, hoping that she would take that as a hint and leave him to continue reading. But apparently the hint was too subtle.

She sat down opposite him, and pulled out some sandwiches. "I prefer reading stories, myself. Visionary fiction in particular, but I like fantasy, paranormal and sci-fi too. Anything to escape this reality."

Josh set his book to one side, and gave Maisy his full attention. "You don't like this reality?" he asked.

Maisy took a bite of her prawn sandwich and shook her head. "Not really," she said after swallowing. "Do you?"

Josh thought for a moment. "Sometimes," he said honestly. "There are some magical parts to living here. But there are a lot of things that I have experienced that I would have rather not have."

"I hear you on that." Maisy shuddered and bit into her sandwich again.

Josh ate some of his own sandwich, and they sat in silence for a while. He wondered why Maisy had decided to begin speaking to him, she never had before, and they had been in a class together for several months already.

"I like your piece so far," Maisy said, studying his canvas that was drying in the sun. "The crystal cave, right? I remember being there."

Josh frowned and looked at the canvas, then looked back at Maisy. "What do you mean? This is a representation of a dream I had last night, how do you know it?"

Maisy smiled. "It's where we came from before this life. These crystals are really children. You knew you were a Crystal Child, right?"

Josh's eyes were wide as he shook his head. He looked at the canvas again. Her words were triggering memories in him. "We were on another planet, we were asked to come here?"

Maisy nodded, then looked around to make sure no one was listening. "Yes. But be careful who you try to speak to about it. There aren't many of us here on this course, but there are more out there. Along with the Indigos and other Earth Angels."

"I have read about Earth Angels," Josh said. "But not about Crystals or Indigos."

"Here," Maisy dug into her bag and pulled out a worn paperback. "This is one of my favourite books. See what you think."

Josh accepted the book from her, and silently read the title. "Is it non-fiction?"

"No, it's a story. But it's a good one. I think you'll like it."

"Thank you. I will return it to you soon. I read very quickly."

Maisy smiled. "No rush. I've read it a million times. Anyway," she got up and brushed the grass off her jeans, screwing up the foil wrapper into a ball and grabbing her bag.

"I need to get on with my piece if I'm going to get out of here on time today."

Josh followed suit, and together they walked back into the art building.

* * *

"Mummy!"

Julie crouched down and opened her arms wide to receive a hug from her youngest, Jerry. She squeezed him hard, and found herself feeling a little emotional over how much she had missed him, even though it had only been a few days.

"How was it?" her husband, Paul, asked, taking her bag into the house for her. "How's, um, er, your friend?"

Julie smiled. He'd forgotten her lie already. "She's great," she said, not helping him out by providing the name he'd forgotten. She picked Jerry up and carried him inside, to where Daniel and Charlotte were playing a video game, seemingly less interested in her return.

"Hey, guys, Mum's home," Paul said. There were two nods but no greetings. Julie shook her head with a smile. At least they hadn't missed her too much.

Paul went to the kitchen and made her a cup of tea, and Julie sat down at the table with Jerry. She watched her husband quietly, wondering if she really had the guts to follow through with her decision. Could she really fly solo with the kids?

The evening passed by in a blur of dinner, bathtime, bedtime stories and unpacking. By the time she and Paul got into bed, Julie was exhausted. But she had to say something.

"Paul," she said quietly, before he turned off the bedside lamp. "We need to talk." From his sigh she guessed that he had been waiting for her to say just that.

"You're not happy," he stated.

A tear rolled down her cheek and she shook her head.

"I know," he said, tears beginning to fall down his own cheeks. "I've felt you pulling away from me, and there is a part of me that wants to hold onto you and not let you go, but I don't think that's the right thing for you, or for me. Things have changed too much, haven't they?"

He looked at her and she nodded, the tears flowing faster. It seemed he was far more aware of the situation than she had given him credit for.

"I just feel stuck," she said, her voice breaking. "I'm not living my purpose, and I need to."

"I'm sorry you feel like you can't do that while being with me," Paul said. "I never intended to make you feel like you had no freedom."

Julie shook her head. "It's not your fault. We just got into this situation slowly. It's what happens when you have children and you work all the time. Things roll on and time disappears and suddenly you realise that you've been living a half-life."

Paul nodded. "Yes, I can understand that. But what are we going to do about the kids? You don't have an income, or a way to support yourself and them."

"I haven't figured any of that out yet."

"Then can I make a suggestion?"

"Of course," Julie said. She was intrigued, it sounded like he had given it all some thought.

"To disrupt the kids as little as possible, let's keep the house, and I'll stay here with them. We can turn the loft into another room for me and you can stay in the bedroom. Or vice versa, I don't mind. Then you go and do what you need to do. Travel, find work, whatever. I can employ someone to look after the kids until I get home, and to clean the house and cook."

Julie's eyes widened. It surprised her that he really had thought it all out. His proposal sounded good and it would be nice not to have to uproot the kids, change schools and move house, but could it work?

"What if we meet other people?" she asked, thinking of the course she'd just attended on Twin Flames.

His face darkened then, and she wondered if his suggestion to stay in the house together was just a way of preventing her from moving forward with someone else.

After too long a pause, he said slowly, "I can't stop you from meeting someone else. I would just ask that you didn't bring them back here, and parade them around in front of the kids."

She leant back into the pillows and frowned. That didn't sound like a situation she wanted to be in. "I need to think it all through," she said, unwilling to commit to his idea. "I need to think about what I want to do next, and whether it makes sense to stay here."

Paul nodded, but she could see he was unhappy that she hadn't agreed straight away. "Where were you really? You weren't at your friend's house, were you?"

"No I wasn't," Julie said, figuring it was pointless lying to him. "I was at a spiritual workshop in London."

"Oh."

"Did you think I was with someone else?" Julie asked, curious.

Paul nodded. "Yes."

"I've never cheated on you, Paul. I wouldn't do that."

"No, you'd just leave me instead," he said bitterly.

Julie sighed. "I'm sorr-"

"I cheated on you. A few months back, when I first felt you being cold toward me. A woman at work has fancied me for years, and she was being flirtatious, so I went with it. We had sex up against the photocopier during a late work session. It made me feel better, so we did it again. It went on for a month, we'd go back to hers during lunch, and after work. Then Charlotte had her accident at school, and I realised what an idiot I was being, risking losing you and the kids."

Julie's heart was beating hard as every word of his rushed confession stabbed her in the chest. She thought back to that time, and recognised now that his behaviour had been different before and after Charlotte's accident, but she'd been too busy to analyse it or even really notice it.

"Aren't you going to say anything" Paul asked finally, after several minutes of silence.

She shook her head. "I'm tired, I need to sleep."

Without another word, Paul switched the lamp off.

"I'm sorry," he said softly into the darkness.

She didn't respond.

Chapter Six

Helen scrolled through the search pages, looking at websites for volunteering abroad. Thanks to Maggie's suggestion, she couldn't get the idea of travelling out of her mind. She had spent some time really going within and deciding what she wanted to do with her life now that she was free of the relationship that had been draining her.

The thought of travelling simply to sightsee didn't really light her up, but going to a place where people needed help, and providing that in whatever way she was able to, really spoke to her.

So now it was just a case of deciding where to go and what to do. Maggie had said she would help pay for the plane ticket, which was incredible. And though Helen knew the practical thing to do would be to work for a while and save up the money to go, she felt a strong desire to get out of the country as soon as possible. She had already sent off for her first-ever passport, and had paid for an express service.

As she clicked on yet another website, and scrolled through photos of smiling children who looked severely malnourished, she wondered how crazy she was. She had never before left the country, not even to go on a family holiday, and yet here she was, thinking of going to a third world country for her first adventure.

"How's it going?"

Helen looked up at Maggie and smiled. "Lots of ideas, no

concrete decisions yet. Any advice or thoughts?"

"You mean where did I See you going?" Maggie shook her head. "Sorry, you're on your own with this one. The decision for this trip needs to come from within, that way, if it goes wrong you won't be blaming me for telling you where to go."

Helen chuckled. "So it's healthier to blame myself instead?"

"Definitely," Maggie replied with a grin. She headed for the kitchen and got a wok and vegetables out. "Was planning to make a stir-fry, hope that's cool. I have quite a bit of reading I want to do tonight, so I thought I'd do something quick."

"Of course," Helen said, getting up from the dining table where she'd been using Maggie's laptop. "Can I help?"

Maggie set her to work, cutting the vegetables into thin strips, and Helen soon lost herself in the menial task.

"I've enjoyed having you here to stay," Maggie said. "It's been nice to have some company."

"It has been great to have girly time," Helen agreed. "It seems crazy for you to be single though, have you thought about internet dating?"

Maggie chuckled. "I think I'm a little bit old to be doing that. No one wants to find an older woman who has visions."

"I think you'd be surprised," Helen said, putting the strips of red pepper into a bowl. "I think there must be an amazing man out there just waiting to snap you up."

Maggie sighed. "There may well be, but obviously it's just not the right time yet for us yet, though…"

"Though?" Helen prompted when her friend lapsed into silence.

"I remember a conversation that took place before this lifetime. Where I was told that I would be with my Twin Flame again. That he was coming back to Earth from his place in the higher realms and that we would find each other, and we would have one more lifetime together. But, well, my lifetime is more than halfway through, and he has yet to materialise."

"Wow, you remember a conversation from before you were born?" Helen had never heard Maggie talk about her life on the Other Side before. She was intrigued.

"Yes, on the Other Side I was a Seer. The Elders and other souls often came to ask me what I could See." Maggie added the vegetables to the sizzling wok and smiled at Helen. "I don't think I would have come back if there hadn't been the promise of meeting my Flame again. So perhaps it was just a promise, just a way to get me to come back to Earth."

"I know you've told me before, but what exactly is a Twin Flame again? I don't quite understand why it's such a big deal. But ever since you mentioned the phrase a little while back, I've seen it everywhere."

"The existence of Twin Flames is why you left your boyfriend. The Flames have been activated, and all those who have one out there somewhere, have become frustrated with their current relationships and now have a desperate need to seek out the one that they feel deeply connected to."

Helen's eyes widened. "You think that I have a Twin Flame? That's why my relationship broke up?"

"It wouldn't surprise me."

"Huh." Helen thought about this while she stirred the veg. "That would be kind of cool, I mean, must be amazing, right?"

"It's intense," Maggie agreed. "But there can be downsides too. Not all Twin Flames are in the right place spiritually, emotionally or physically to be able to maintain the relationship, and they find themselves separated. And when that happens," she shook her head and sighed. "It can be devastating."

Helen laid the table for the two of them and thought about what Maggie had said. "I don't think I want to focus on it," she said once they were sat with heaped platefuls. "I think I'd rather focus on myself, and on my mission to serve others. If I happen to meet my Flame along the way, that's cool. If not," she shrugged. "That's also cool."

"Very wise words," Maggie said. "And I know that you

will be all the happier for having made that decision."

"Are you not happy?" Helen asked. Her friend always seemed to have it all together.

Maggie thought about it for a while. "I am, most days. When I'm running my workshops and doing readings, I feel great. But in the dark, quiet of the night, when it's just me and my thoughts, I find it difficult to find the light within, to see the good in the fact that I have been on my own for so many years. The feeling has been getting stronger with each passing year since my twin brother died."

Helen felt tears gathering in her eyes, but she knew that her friend wouldn't want her pity. "You had a twin brother?"

Maggie smiled. "Yes, his name was Adrian. He was amazing. He died of cancer a few years ago."

"I'm so sorry."

"It's okay, I had many wonderful years growing up with him. And besides, his spirit lives on. After all, there is no such thing as death. Not really. It's just a transition from one form into another."

Helen continued eating quietly for a while. She thought back to when she lost her mother when she was a child. She hadn't understood death then. She thought her mum had just gone away for a while, but she would be back. It took quite some time before she accepted and came to terms with the fact that she would never see her mother again.

"Where do they go? The people we lose?"

"Home," Maggie said. "They go home."

Helen sighed. "There have been so many times when I have wanted to go home too."

"I think that's true of most Earth Angels. It's not easy, being on Earth." Maggie reached over and patted her hand. "You're doing well, just start focussing on finding your passion, what you love. The rest will happen effortlessly."

"I think that's been the problem. I was so fixated on finding a person to love me, that it didn't occur to me to find what I loved to do, or where I loved to be, or to even learn how to love myself."

"I think most people are the same. When we look for happiness or love outside of ourselves, before finding it within, whatever we find will never be sustainable."

Helen finished her meal and set her fork down. "That was lovely," she said. "I'll do the washing up tonight."

Maggie yawned and stretched. "That would be amazing. I need to do some reading then get an early night, I have a few clients booked in tomorrow at the crystal shop in town."

"I'm going to carry on doing some research," Helen said, taking their plates to the sink.

"Just don't spend too long researching. Find something that feels good, then go for it. Don't overthink it. Go with your intuition."

Helen turned the hot tap on to fill the sink. "I will, I promise," she said over the sound of the running water.

Maggie brought their glasses over to the sink, kissed Helen on the side of the head, then said goodnight and retreated to her bedroom, leaving Helen to wash the dishes and stare out of the window into the dusk.

* * *

"Josh! Are you still asleep? You need to sort out an alarm clock, this is getting ridiculous. What time were you up until last night?"

Josh opened one eye blearily in response to his mother's barrage of questions and exclamations. As sleep receded, the memory of the previous evening came into his mind and he sat bolt upright, making his mum jump.

"Josh, are you okay?" she asked, peering at his pale face.

He grabbed the book from his bedside table, and clutched it to his chest. "Yes, thank you for waking me up, I need to get to college quickly."

His mother frowned, but stepped out of the way as he leapt out of bed and started throwing his clothes on. Minutes later, he was dashing out of the door, stopping only briefly to receive the sandwich and kiss from his bewildered mum.

He had finished reading the book that Maisy had lent him, and he had to talk to her about it. He resonated so strongly with the story, and with the characters, that he knew that it couldn't be merely a work of fiction. It just wasn't possible.

He bounced up and down in his seat on the bus, and was at the door waiting to jump off before the vehicle had come to a full stop outside the college.

He ran to the art department, skidding to a stop by the bench in the gardens outside when he saw Maisy sitting there in the sunshine, sketching something in her notepad.

"Maisy!" he said, throwing himself down on the bench next to her.

"Josh!" she replied with a laugh. "You look like you're about to burst, what's up?"

"It's real, isn't it? The story in the book you lent me, it's just got to be real, I mean, I dreamt of the world the Crystal Children came from."

Maisy smiled and showed him her sketch. It was of a garden full of golden statues.

Josh gasped in recognition. "The Atlantis Garden. I remember being there. I remember seeing the statues. You were there too."

"Yes, the Atlantis Garden was my favourite. Not that we spent much time at the Academy, after all, our knowledge is vast. But we did need to learn a few things about being on Earth, and about how to keep the magic of our light alive."

Josh's eyes were wide. "This is incredible. What crystal are you?"

"Citrine," Maisy said. She looked down at her predominantly yellow and orange clothing. "Can't you tell?" she teased. "You?"

Josh answered before he'd even realised he knew the answer. "Blue tourmaline." He frowned at his own words. "That's really weird, I didn't know that until the very moment

I just said it. But I have a piece of blue tourmaline, I bought it two years ago, and I've carried it in my pocket ever since." He pulled out the small crystal, and as the sunlight shone on it, the light blue crystal lit up his palm.

"That's a beautiful piece," Maisy said. She pulled her necklace out from under her t-shirt. She showed him her citrine pendant.

"So am I the first Crystal Child you've met?" she asked.

"I don't know. I wasn't even really aware of the concept until you told me about it the other day, and then reading this book, well, I think I might have met lots of Crystals, Indigos and Earth Angels already, but I just didn't realise it."

"Probably," Maisy agreed.

They sat in silence for a moment, as people rushed past them to get to their classes on time.

"So what now? I mean, in the story it says that we came here to help the world, to make a difference. So how do we do that?"

Maisy smiled. "I like to think that we do it in little ways, every day. Every time we smile at a stranger, create a piece of art, commit a random act of kindness – we're living our purpose on this Earth."

"What is our purpose?"

"To love, to inspire, to be joyful." Maisy shrugged. "That's my thoughts, at least. We're here to help people to realise that there's more to life than they think."

Josh thought about her words for a while. He'd always had an inner knowing that there was more to be understood about life, but he hadn't been able to grasp it before. The idea of inspiring people to wake up to the beauty of the world was both exciting and terrifying and overwhelming all at the same time.

Maisy covered his hand with hers. "Try not to overthink it. If you think of all that needs to happen, you will get overwhelmed and stuck. And you won't know what to do first. In truth, there is nothing you need to do in this life. Just being yourself, living your life is enough."

"It doesn't seem like enough," Josh said. "After all, painting pictures of still life and creating sculptures out of clay doesn't seem like the kind of thing that will wake people up and make a difference in the world."

"That's where you're wrong. Art makes a huge difference, as does music and literature. The energetic vibration of what we create makes a big difference to the world as a whole. We can uplift, inspire, and cause a range of emotions to be felt through our work. So if you infuse the intention of love, light and Awakening into your pieces, you will be fulfilling your mission."

Josh thought about this for a while. He did love to create art, and he loved the idea that his work could inspire or uplift others. But would it really make a difference? Was it really enough?

"We're late for class," Maisy said, and Josh looked around to realise that they were alone in the courtyard.

"Nothing new for me," Josh said, standing up, then offering his hand to Maisy. She smiled and took it, and together they went to their first class. Josh's mind was whirring with all the new information he'd just learnt. He decided there and then that he didn't want to do just small things. He wanted to make a big difference. He just wasn't quite sure how yet.

Chapter Seven

"Your leg is healing well, I think it might be time to try and get you on your feet, move around a bit."

Tadhg raised an eyebrow at the nurse, then turned away from her and stared down at the sheets.

"You can't stay in this bed forever," the nurse cajoled, her playful tone irritating Tadhg to the core.

"You're right," Tadhg agreed, looking up at her and catching her by surprise. "Because if I stayed here forever I would have to put up with your ridiculous cheerfulness, and I may go insane."

The nurse pursed her lips, and Tadhg couldn't tell if she was upset or if she was about to burst out laughing. And neither did he care. "I'll get up when I'm ready," he said. "And not a moment sooner."

The nurse nodded, trying to look serious, but Tadhg could tell she wanted to giggle. He waved her away, he couldn't bear her enthusiastic energy any more.

She left the room, and he resumed his miserable activity of staring at the window blinds. They didn't even have the courtesy to open them for him to look outside. He picked up the TV remote and switched on the tiny black box. He found the news channel then stared at the depressing footage of wars raging in distant parts of the world, people being raped, murdered or going missing, and the general demise of the human population. He settled back into his pillows, feeling comfortable for the first time in days.

Lunchtime finally rolled around, and Tadhg's stomach growled when the smell of food reached him. He looked down at the lunch tray in dismay. First they chopped his leg off without asking, now they were trying to poison him.

"What is this?" he asked the nurse in disgust, poking the congealed mess with his plastic fork. "You're either trying to starve me or poison me, I can't figure out which."

"It does look a bit dire, doesn't it?" the nurse agreed. "It drives me mad that they serve such terrible food to people who are sick, when really, they need food full of vitamins and nutrients to get them well again." She shrugged. "Doctors don't put much stock in diet having any effect on your health, which is crazy, don't you think?"

Tadhg was unimpressed by her speech. "I don't care about healthy food, I would just like something edible." He threw his fork down without taking a single bite. "Just take it away. I think I'd rather starve."

The nurse frowned but complied with his request. His stomach growled loudly then, making her frown deepen. "I can see if there's anything else I-"

"Just take it away," Tadhg said, cutting her off. "I doubt they'll have anything else that is actually edible."

He waited until she'd left the room before allowing the tear to fall that had been threatening. So he didn't cry when he found out he'd lost his leg, but the idea of having no lunch had reduced him to tears? What the hell was wrong with him?

He turned his focus back to the news channel, and tried to block out the hunger pangs that threatened to take over his whole body. About half an hour later, he saw the door opening and sighed. Was she ever going to leave him alone?

She came in, a beaming smile on her face, and a brown paper package in her hands. She put his tray back across his lap, then presented him with it. Before he could demand to know what was inside, the most delicious smell rose up, and he ripped it open to find a large tomato and mozzarella sandwich and a big cup of soup. He pulled the lid off the cup and the smell of curried parsnip filled his nostrils, making him sigh.

He looked up at the nurse, who seemed pleased by his reaction.

"You need to eat," she said softly. "So I used my break to go to my favourite deli and get this for you. Sorry it took me a while."

Tadhg swallowed his emotions, determined not to cry in front of her. Instead, he nodded, and muttered a quiet 'Thanks' before tucking into the sandwich.

She smiled, nodded and then left the room. Tadhg felt an unfamiliar feeling rise up in his chest, as he slowly chewed the soft white bread and the tangy, juicy tomatoes. It took him a while to work out what it was, but then it finally dawned on him.

It was the feeling of gratitude.

* * *

Sherrie looked at herself in the mirror and was amazed at her reflection staring back at her. She looked professional, but somehow, still like herself.

"What do you think?" she asked Jim as he walked past the doorway of the bedroom. He paused for a second, barely glanced at her then grunted 'Fine'.

Sherrie sighed and looked back at the mirror. He had been difficult to live with ever since she'd accepted the new job with Fishy Friends. She wished he could be excited for her, for both of them, seeing as it would mean she'd have a steady income for once, and may even mean that he could give up the job he hated and concentrate on a project he was passionate about.

But instead, he'd decided to focus on the negatives of it all. The fact that she would be doing a lot of travelling, and that she would be put into some potentially risky situations.

Her heartbeat sped up at the idea of actually saving the lives of ocean creatures. It was what she was there for, after all.

She glanced at the clock on the bedside table, and realised she needed to get a move on if she was to be on time for her first day.

She threw a few necessities in her handbag, attached her lucky mermaid keyring to the zipper, then slung it over her shoulder, and gave her reflection one last look. "You can do this," she whispered to herself, trying to calm the nervous butterflies fluttering in her stomach.

She left the bedroom, and called out 'goodbye' to Jim, but if he heard her, then he didn't bother replying. With a sigh she shook off his negativity and made her way out of the apartment to her car.

Once she was on the highway and had her favourite music playing, Sherrie felt much better. She knew that this was the beginning of a whole new chapter in her life, and she hoped that at some point, Jim would come round and see it from her perspective.

When she arrived at the offices, she was surprised to see how low-key the building looked, the exterior gave nothing away of what went on inside.

She showed her pass to security, who waved her through and wished her luck. Then she parked her car and headed toward the simple modern building.

"Good morning," the secretary called out when she entered the foyer. She headed for the cheerful woman, as she wasn't completely sure where to go.

"Hi, it's my first day here and I don't know where I'm meant to be."

"You must be Sherrie. Welcome to Fishy Friends. You will be looked after by Fin today, I will just call up and let him know that you've arrived."

"Fin?" Sherrie repeated, a smile on her face. Quite the appropriate name for a guy fighting for the lives and rights of sea life.

"Yes, Fin," the secretary replied with a smile. She picked up the phone and dialed. After a moment, she spoke to someone, and notified them of Sherrie's arrival.

"He will be down in just a moment. Please take a seat," she said, pointing to the chairs surrounding a low coffee table covered in magazines. Sherrie nodded and went to sit down. She picked up one of the magazines, and flicked through, but the gruesome images of whales and sharks and other creatures being harmed was too much and she set it down, now feeling even queasier than before.

"Sherrie," a warm voice said, pulling her out of her thoughts. She looked up into the warm blue eyes of a beautiful man with shoulder length curly brown hair.

"Yes," she said, feeling a little dazzled by how beautiful he was.

"Welcome, I'm Fin," he said, holding out his hand. She shook it, hoping that her own palm wasn't too sweaty.

"Come with me. We're in the offices at the top, amazing view of the ocean from there."

Sherrie nodded, grabbed her bag and followed him to the elevator.

"We thought today we would just show you the ropes, the daily stuff that goes on, and then as projects come up, we'll take you out into the field, and then when you feel comfortable, we'll start doing the filming stuff. We're eager to add more videos to our YouTube channel, we want to raise the awareness of these issues as much as we can."

Sherrie nodded. "That all sounds good," she said. "I'm excited to get started."

Fin smiled. "Excellent, I'm sure you will enjoy working with us, we're a good bunch."

Sherrie smiled back. "I'm sure I will."

Chapter Eight

"You don't have to do this."
Julie looked into Paul's eyes, as he pleaded for her not to leave. "Yes I do," she said softly, placing more of her clothing into a suitcase. "If I stay, then we'll end up carrying on as normal. And that's no longer an option."
Paul sighed in frustration. "But why do you have to leave at all? I'm sorry about the affair, it won't ever happen again. I understand now why I did it, and how wrong it was. I love you, I want to be with you and the kids. I don't want us to separate."
"I know you don't. And I will probably always feel love for you, but right now, I'm not in love with you, and I'm not happy. And I haven't been either of those things for quite some time. So things need to change. I will take the kids to stay with a friend for now until I can find a job and rent us somewhere. Then when the divorce has gone through and the house is sold, I will sort out something more permanent."
"Or you could make it really easy and just stay. You can still get a job if you want to, and go travelling, you don't have to leave, take the kids away, it's not necessary. Besides, I'm not happy with you taking them out of school before the end of the term."
"It is necessary. We cannot move forward if we're still in each other's pockets, Paul. It's just not possible. And I've already sorted it out with their school. I explained the situation, they were very understanding."

He stormed out of the room, and she continued to pack, folding her clothes as small as possible, as she knew she'd only fit so much in her car, especially with everything the kids would need. Thank goodness Violet and Greg had a large pod they could spare for a few weeks.

She finished filling her suitcase, then zipped it up and heaved it off the bed onto the floor. She'd asked the kids to start packing their things, but knowing them, they would only think to pack the most impractical items, and forget to pack their underwear and socks.

She headed to their bedrooms, and found a whirlwind of chaos. She sighed and started to tidy up, wondering where the three of them had disappeared to. She picked up Jerry's favourite stuffed zebra, and then sat on the bed and felt her eyes well up. Though she was sure that she was making the right decision for herself, she couldn't help but worry if it was really the right thing for the kids. They had a beautiful home here, they were used to having whatever they needed or wanted, and she was going to be taking them away to live in a cabin in the woods for a few weeks until she could work out how to support herself and them.

Was she crazy?

She hugged the zebra to her chest, and for the first time since she'd made her decision to leave, and found out about Paul's affair, she allowed the tears to fall.

"Mum, are you okay?"

Julie quickly wiped away her tears on her sleeve and smiled at her middle child, Daniel. "Yes, baby, I'm fine. Where's Jerry and Charlotte? I thought I asked you guys to get packing?

"They're playing ball outside with Dad."

Anything to distract them from packing to leave, Julie thought. She smiled at her son. "Okay, that's cool. We will have to get a move on though, I told Violet we'd be arriving in a few days."

"Are we going to have to change schools?" Daniel asked,

his eyes wide.

Julie patted the bed and he went to sit next to her. "Maybe," she said, putting her arm around his wiry frame. "It will all depend on where I manage to get work. I'm not sure what I will be doing yet."

"I don't want you and Dad to split up, or to have to move schools, but I would like to see you happy. Will leaving here make you happy?"

Julie felt the tears begin to fall at the words of her wise eight-year-old son.

"Yes, I think it will make me happy," she said. "I'm sorry if it takes a little while to adjust to all the changes though."

Daniel shrugged. "It'll just be like a new adventure."

"Yes, it will. Now, how about you and I go join the others and play ball?"

Daniel nodded, Julie set the zebra down, and they went outside to play in the sunshine.

* * *

"It feels too soon to be saying goodbye," Maggie said, as she helped Helen to get her rucksack out of the car.

"I know," Helen said. "I've really enjoyed staying with you, but I know this is the right thing to do."

"I know it is too. You're going to have the most amazing time. Just make sure you find a computer or a phone and get in touch with me, let me know how you're getting on, okay?"

"Yes, Mum," Helen joked. She pulled her friend into a tight hug to show she was kidding. "I'll miss you," she said. "Thank you for everything."

"Anytime. You are always welcome in my home."

Helen pulled away and picked up her rucksack, trying to make it look light and effortless, but in truth it took all of her strength to heave it onto her back. She wished she had been able to pack just a little bit lighter.

She said goodbye to her friend and then made her way into

the airport, to the check-in desk. She was a little apprehensive, having never done any of this before in her life, but she'd watched enough movies to know roughly how it all worked.

Once she'd checked in and her rucksack had rolled away on the conveyor belt, she felt a little bit lost. She followed the signs to the gate, and after getting through security, where she felt like she'd been a little violated by the pat-down search, she made her way to a café to get a hot drink and wait until her flight was boarding.

She settled down with her hot chocolate and sipped it slowly while reading the guide she'd bought for her trip.

After much research online, she'd come across a programme in Nepal, where they were helping people to rebuild their homes and businesses after the terrible earthquakes in 2015. Despite it being two years since the disaster, there were still many Nepalese people living in temporary housing and shelters.

She folded her paper napkin into a small square, then opened it up and refolded it, then started to shred it into small pieces, while staring into space.

"Worried about flying?"

Helen looked up and focussed on a face across from her. She'd been so lost in her thoughts she hadn't noticed him sit down.

She followed his gaze to the shredded napkin and she laughed. "Well, I don't know, I've never flown anywhere before, so I have no idea what to expect. Should I be worried?"

The stranger shook his head. "Nah, flying is pretty safe these days. I've flown all over the world and lived to tell the tale."

"Really? All over the world? What do you do?" The nosey question was out of Helen's mouth before she had the chance to reign herself in. "I'm sorry, that's a rather direct question. Please ignore it if you want."

He chuckled. "It's cool. I'm a web designer. I work entirely online, and I have clients all over the world. So I don't have an office, I just work from my laptop wherever I am."

"Wow, that sounds great."

He shrugged. "It's great to be able to set up my office wherever I want, after all, working from a beach in Bali or a retreat in Thailand is amazing, but sometimes I think it would be quite nice to stay in one place for more than a few months."

"I guess. I think settling down is overrated though."

"Is that what you're running away from?"

Helen laughed. "Yes, I guess I am. I just recently split up with my boyfriend. And I've decided to volunteer in Nepal, help build houses, that kind of thing."

His eyes widened. "Now that sounds like an amazing thing to do. You're making me feel quite selfish."

Helen frowned. "That's not my intention. This is the first time I've ever done anything like this, it's not like I'm Mother Theresa or anything. There was just something about the programme that spoke to me, so I trusted my gut and went for it."

"Still sounds amazing."

"I hope so." Helen sipped her hot chocolate that was now lukewarm. "Where are you off to this time?"

The man leaned back in his chair. "I'm off to Australia for a month. I have a big client there, and it seemed like a good idea to meet in person, then spend a little time in Sydney, seeing the sights. I'm staying with a friend, so costs are fairly low."

"Australia. Wow. That's quite a commute."

He shrugged. "Meeting the client is just an excuse really. I've just always wanted to go there. I've felt drawn there all my life, but never really understood why."

"Maybe you had a past life there," Helen suggested.

"You believe in that? In past lives?" he asked.

"Yes, I do. Don't you?"

"I do, but I've not met many others who do."

"Really? Even though you've travelled all over the world? I have many friends who believe in it. One of them is a psychic medium who talks to people who have crossed over."

His eyebrows shot up, and he set his coffee down. "Does she do readings? I'd love to get a reading done when I get back from Australia."

"Sure," Helen said, pulling a pen and a piece of paper from her handbag. "Here's her number," she said, scribbling Maggie's name and phone number on it then passing it to him.

"Thanks," he said, placing the paper inside his wallet. "I'm Steve, by the way."

"Helen," she said, leaning over to shake the hand he offered. "Nice to meet you, Steve."

"Helen. That's a lovely name," he said, making Helen blush.

She shrugged. "I always thought it was a little old-fashioned."

"I think it suits you," Steve said as he bit into the chocolate brownie in front of him, making Helen feel hungry.

"I might need to go get one of those," she said, ignoring his compliment. "Does it taste as good as it looks?"

"Yeah, it's quite a good brownie. Not a patch on my homemade ones, but pretty good."

"You make brownies?" Helen asked, finding him more intriguing by the minute.

"Yes, I like baking. My mother was a terrible cook, so I learnt how to bake so that I had something decent to eat after the terrible dinners she forced on me."

Helen laughed. She got her purse out then stood up. "Do you want anything?"

Steve shook his head. "No, but I'll save your spot for you."

"Thanks." Helen headed for the counter, smiling to herself. It was a shame that Steve was headed to Australia and she was headed to Nepal. She wouldn't have minded spending more time with him. She bought another hot chocolate and a brownie, then headed back to her seat, only to find Steve gathering his things.

"My flight is boarding," he said, making her heart sink.

"Here's my card though, if you want to meet up for a drink when we're both back in the country, just let me know, I'd love to know how your house-building adventures go."

Helen took the card from him and scanned the details on it. "I'd like that."

Steve smiled, then turned and walked toward the gates.

Everything in Helen was screaming for her to follow him, to not let him get on a plane to the other side of the world. But the sensible part of her won over and she sat down and ate her brownie and drank her hot chocolate, all the while not tasting any of it.

Chapter Nine

"I can do it!"

The nurse, who Tadhg had finally learnt was called Lily, nodded and stepped back, allowing him some space.

He defiantly lifted the crutches to move forward, but tried to go too far and got off balance. He started to pitch forward and had no way of steadying himself. A pair of slim arms shot out to steady him, and he was surprised at the strength in them. But instead of expressing gratitude for her saving him from face-planting on the floor, he turned and snapped at her.

"Let go of me. I can do it by myself."

"Of course," Lily said, letting go and stepping back again.

Tadhg momentarily regretted causing the look of upset that crossed her face, but soon forgot his regret in the next second when a shooting pain went up his good leg, making it crumple and he collapsed to the floor, hitting his stump and making him scream out in pain.

"Would you like any help?" Lily asked, still standing away from him.

Breathing hard, he glared up at her, but to his horror, tears formed in response to the pain, and started running down his face.

The look on her face softened, and she slowly moved toward him. "It'll get easier," she whispered, holding out a tissue to him.

He took the tissue and wiped his eyes.

"How do you figure that? It's not like my leg will eventually grow back."

"No, but your good leg will grow stronger. And when everything is fully healed, you could get a prosthetic fitted."

"Oh great, I can drag a bit of metal and plastic around with me as well then."

"I think you can get yourself up," Lily said, her tone becoming annoyed. "I have other patients who are eager to get well and get back on their feet."

With that, she left, leaving Tadhg on the floor with his mouth open.

Enraged, he grabbed the crutches and somehow pulled himself back up onto his good leg. He wasn't anywhere near the bed or a chair, so he was going to have to walk. His irritation at being left to get on with it fuelled him enough to master the crutches and make his way to the door. With a bit of hopping about and leaning on the wall, he managed to open the door and step out into the corridor. The hospital was quiet at that time, in between visiting hours, and no one stopped him or questioned him as he slowly made his way down the hall, looking for Lily. He wanted to give her a piece of his mind for leaving him. What if he'd been stuck there?

He peered through the window of the room two doors down, but the person there was asleep. He made his way down the hall, his leg ached from the effort, but his irritation pushed him on. Finally, he peered into a room and saw Lily feeding a patient, and laughing with them as she did so.

He managed to open the door, and she looked up in surprise at him as he leaned on the doorframe.

"I can't believe you just left me there," he said.

She frowned. "Well, you were hardly helpless. Look at how far you've just walked."

The other patient watched the exchange with interest, while slowly chewing their food.

"That's not the point! What if I couldn't get up? Would you have eventually come back to help me?"

"Probably," Lily sighed. "Why don't you come and sit down, I'll get a wheelchair. You probably shouldn't walk back as well, you'll wear yourself out."

Feeling vindicated, Tadhg took a chair next to the bedside, and Lily stood up.

"Here," she said, handing him the spoon and bowl. "Could you finish feeding George while I get the wheelchair?"

Tadhg looked down at the spoon and bowl in horror, but with the patient looking on, didn't feel like he could refuse. Lily left the room and he had no choice but to continue feeding the unidentifiable chunks to the incapacitated man who had both arms in casts.

"So," he said, feeling awkward. "What happened to you?"

"You should know," George said, raising an eyebrow. "You're the one that caused the accident."

Tadhg dropped the spoon on the floor. "You were in the same accident? How did you know I caused it?"

"They said the guy overtaking lost his leg, so I assumed it was you. I was in the vehicle behind the one that hit you head on. The impact flipped me over and my arms got crushed because I wasn't wearing a seatbelt and got flung around."

"But they'll be okay? Your arms?" Tadhg asked, feeling a little bit guilty that he had caused the man's injuries.

"Eventually. Had quite a bit of surgery on them, but yeah, providing there's not too much nerve damage, all should be okay in a few months."

Tadhg nodded, then leaned down to pick the spoon up off the floor. "Uh, do you want more?"

George shook his head. "No thanks, I'll wait for Lily to come back if you don't mind."

"Sure," Tadhg said, relieved to be able to put the bowl down. "I'm uh, sorry about what happened."

George raised an eyebrow. "Yeah, somehow, considering your attitude just now, I kind of doubt that."

Tadhg felt his temper flare up at the stranger's words. How dare he rebuff his apology?

"But knowing that you lost your leg, and that you haven't had a single visitor since you've been in here, I feel sorrier for you than I do for myself. So there's no need to apologise."

Tadhg blinked, unsure of how to respond. He felt indignant, he didn't need this man's sympathy, and he was angry that this complete stranger knew that he'd had no visitors, but mostly, he was just feeling very sorry for himself.

"Are you ready, Tadhg?"

He looked around to see Lily waiting there with a wheelchair. He nodded and without a word she helped him up and into the chair.

"See you again, Tadhg," George said as he was wheeled out of the room,

"I'll be back to continue our date in a moment, George," Lily said over her shoulder. "I'll get you some food too," she said to Tadhg as she pushed him down the hall back to his room.

"Don't bother," he said. "The food just gets worse with every meal, and I'm afraid I don't have the stomach for it today."

"I could pop out to get you more food from the deli if you want," Lily suggested.

Tadhg felt himself melt for a moment. The lunch she'd bought him from the deli had been the most amazing meal he'd had since coming back from the dead. But he hated feeling indebted to anyone.

"Fine," he said. "But I'll give you the money for it this time. I don't need you to do me any favours."

Though he couldn't see her face, he could feel her smiling when she said "Sure."

They reached his room and she helped him back to bed, then put the chair in the corner of the room. "I need to finish helping George, then I'll pop out to get you some food. Why don't you find a nice depressing news channel to watch while I'm gone?"

Tadhg raised an eyebrow at her sarcastic tone, but grabbed

the remote control in defiance and did just that.

*   *   *

What had she been thinking?

She'd never even been to France on a school trip before now, why on earth had she decided to travel by herself all the way to Nepal to help build houses? She'd never even picked up a hammer before either.

While Helen sat on a bench outside the airport, waiting for the person from the volunteer programme to pick her up, she wondered if she should just go straight back to the airline desk and get on the next flight back home.

Because as she looked around her at the sights, and breathed in the air thick with unfamiliar smells, she knew she must have made a gigantic mistake.

After fending off yet another offer of a ride from a taxi driver, she stood up and grabbed her rucksack off the floor, and was about to go back into the airport when she heard her name being called. She turned around to see a young guy running up to her, waving a piece of paper.

"Helen," he said again when he stopped suddenly in front of her.

Taken aback by his sudden arrival and the weird wave of familiarity that washed over her as she looked into his eyes, all Helen could do was nod.

"I'm so sorry I'm late," he continued, catching his breath. His accent was soft, but Helen was sure it was American.

"The minibus broke down about ten minutes away, and getting it fixed was taking forever so I thought I should run to meet you, just in case you were worried I had forgotten about you." He smiled apologetically. "Were you heading inside to call the headquarters to see where we were?"

"Um, yes," Helen lied, finally finding her voice. "It's okay, I haven't been waiting that long."

"Oh good, I'm afraid we'll have to get a taxi back to the

headquarters, is that okay?"

"Of course." Helen watched him approach the first taxi in line, then effortlessly load her massive rucksack into the boot before opening the door for her. "Thanks," she murmured, getting into the tiny vehicle.

He introduced himself as Chad – definitely American, Helen thought to herself – and he kept up a steady stream of chatter all the way to the headquarters, pointing out sights along the way, including buildings and monuments that had been destroyed during the 2015 quake.

Helen nodded and responded appropriately when required, but she barely took in a word he said. She was having a very intense inner dialogue with herself. Part of her looked around at the scenes of poverty around her, and wanted to get the hell out of there, go back to Maggie's beautifully decorated home and hide. Another part of her ached to make a difference, to help in whatever way she could, and yet another part of her was just idly wondering what Chad looked like naked.

"I'm sorry," Chad said suddenly. "This is all probably way too much for you to take in after a long journey. I'll just stop talking for a bit."

Helen looked at Chad, and realised that it must have been obvious she really wasn't paying attention. "No, it's fine, I'm sorry, my mind was elsewhere, I was wondering if I'd made a mistake." The words were out of her mouth before she could stop them, and she instantly regretted them when she saw the look on Chad's face.

"What kind of mistake?"

Helen blinked, wishing she weren't so tired. "I don't know how to build houses. And this is the first time I've ever left England. I really don't know if I can do this."

Chad smiled. "Trust me, nearly all our volunteers go through this exact same phase. Just give me two weeks, and I promise that you will be just fine."

Helen nodded, but was still uncertain. She figured that if

she just stayed two weeks, it would be a kind of working holiday, and would at least be a break from her normal life.

Whatever normal was now.

They pulled up in front of a building that looked like it would have been condemned if it had been back in the UK.

"Here we are," Chad said cheerfully, hopping out of the taxi after giving the driver a generous tip.

Helen followed slowly, and joined Chad on the steps where he stood with her rucksack slung over his shoulder.

He took her into the building and she filled out some paperwork at the front desk, before being shown to her room, which wasn't quite as bad as she had imagined it might be. The sheets looked clean, at least.

Chad set her rucksack on the floor, and then stood awkwardly by the door. He was sticking to his promise of not saying too much, but now he just looked uncomfortable with her silence.

"I'm sorry," she said finally. "This is all a bit overwhelming, and I still think I may have made a mistake."

Chad smiled. "I'll leave you to get settled in, I have no doubt that you'll be fine, it's just a lot to take in straight away."

Helen nodded, and without another word, he left the room, pulling the door closed behind him. Helen sank down onto the bed and sighed. She pulled her phone out of her pocket and switched it on, then logged into the Wi-Fi. Part of her was surprised that they even had Wi-Fi, but she was too grateful to wonder about it. She opened her emails, and found one from Maggie, saying she hoped she was safe. She replied quickly, but kept it light, she didn't want her friend worrying about her.

Once she'd done that, she went over to the window and looked out at the alien landscape beyond. Seeing the devastation up close had affected her. Seeing things on the TV or computer screen from far away just didn't have the same impact as seeing it for real.

But could she really make any kind of difference? In that moment she didn't think so, but then again, she was exhausted.

She went back over to the bed and lay down on top of the covers. She closed her eyes, and within moments, was fast asleep.

Chapter Ten

"Where are you going?"

Josh looked up at his mum as he put on a light jacket. "I'm meeting Maisy from college. We're going for a walk in the park."

His mother raised her eyebrows. "You're going for a walk in the park with a girl?"

Josh heard the insinuation in his mother's voice and grinned. "She's just a friend, Mum, it's not like that. We have a lot in common, and there are things we want to talk about. Spiritual things."

His mum nodded but didn't look convinced. "Okay, well, have fun, but try to be back early. Just because it's Sunday tomorrow doesn't mean that you shouldn't get an early night. You need to get into a better routine, so I don't have to drag you out of bed every morning for college."

"Okay," Josh said, kissing her on the cheek before dashing out the door. He jogged down the road to the park entrance, where Maisy was sat waiting for him on a bench.

"Sorry I'm late," Josh said, a little out of breath.

Maisy shook her head. "No biggie, I was a bit early, so I decided to do some sketching." She held up her notepad, and Josh's eyes widened as he recognised the scene she had sketched out in great detail. "The main hall?"

"Yes," Maisy said with a smile. "That's Linen and that's Aria," she said, pointing to the two figures on the stage.

"Yes, I remember them. I've been having lots of dreams recently, but I don't know if they're really memories or if they're my mind trying to recreate scenes from the book."

"Do they feel real?" Maisy asked. "Can you remember all the sounds and smells and sights when you wake up?"

"Yes, they're really vivid."

"Then they're probably memories," Maisy said, tucking her notepad back into her rucksack and standing up. Together they went through the park gates toward the rolling green lawns.

"I have quite vivid dreams too," Maisy said. "I dream of our home planet. For a long time, I really just wanted to go home, but now I know that we're here for an important reason, and that one day we will be allowed to go home again, I figure I may as well just enjoy being here, just enjoy the ride."

"That's a good way to look at it," Josh said. They walked for a few minutes in silence, then found a quiet grassy area surrounded by trees. Maisy put her jumper down on the grass then sat on top of it, and Josh took his jacket off and did the same. The clouds parted a little, and the late morning sun shone through the leaves onto their faces. Maisy closed her eyes and turned her face up to the light.

"Feels good," she murmured. "The warmth reminds me of home."

Josh smiled. "Being on Earth isn't so bad. I mean, there's lots of fun things we can do. I really enjoy college, getting to play with different mediums and create things from raw materials."

"I know, but there are so many dark things on this planet too, it hurts to see them, to feel them."

Josh shrugged. "I avoid watching or reading the news. I stay away from negative people and situations, I try to remain positive at all times. Even when there's bad things that happen around me that I can't avoid, I try to look at them in a positive light."

Maisy turned and looked at him, a smile on her face. "I

hope you manage to keep that optimism. Most of us lose that early on, and spend the rest of our lives trying to get it back."

"I'll do my best," Josh promised.

"So what did you want to do today?" Maisy asked.

"I was thinking about what you said the other day, about small acts of kindness, about them making a big difference, and I thought maybe we could make a concentrated effort to do them." Josh pulled out some items from his bag. "So I have paper, pens, and my savings. I was thinking we could write some little notes to give people, and pay for random things, or buy some flowers and give them to people." He shrugged. "I would just like to make lots of people smile today."

Maisy grinned. "That sounds brilliant." She reached out for a pen and some paper, and got her notepad out to lean on. As she began to write notes, Josh admired how her hair seemed to have yellow and orange highlights in it when the sun shone on her head.

Maisy looked up after a moment and caught him staring. He blushed a little and looked down at his own paper. He started writing positive notes, which told the recipient how beautiful they were, and how they deserved to be happy and joyful.

Once they had a decent pile of notes between them, they decided to go to the market and get some flowers, then begin their rampage of kindness.

Giggling, they set off across the park, and raced each other to the flower stand. Josh held back a little and let Maisy win. The look of joy on her face was worth it.

"First date?" the florist asked.

Josh and Maisy looked at each other and giggled again. Maisy shook her head. "No, we're just friends. We're buying flowers to give to random people to make their day."

The florist smiled. "That sounds like a great idea. Can I recommend the gerberas? They're easy to split so you can give out single ones, and I have them in all different colours."

Josh nodded. "Sounds good, we'll take ten please."

"Tell you what, I'll give you twenty for the price of ten, then you can make twice as many people happy." She wrapped them up for them, and Josh handed her the money while Maisy took the bouquet. They both thanked her several times, then headed for the high street.

They stood off to one side for a while, watching everyone rushing past. Josh was feeling a bit nervous about approaching complete strangers on the street. He'd never done anything like it before.

"Let's do this," Maisy whispered. She handed him the bunch of flowers, and took a single one out of the middle. She plucked a random note from the bundle, then bounded up to an unsuspecting shopper sat on a bench, looking a little miserable, and held the note and bright orange flower out to him.

He looked up at her, and when he saw her smile, he couldn't help but smile back. He took the gifts offered and read the note, his smile growing wider.

"Have a beautiful day," Maisy said, loud enough for Josh to hear from where he was rooted to the spot. Maisy skipped back to Josh. "That was fun," she said. "Your turn now." She pulled another single flower from the bunch and a note from her pocket, then handed them to him. Josh looked down at the bright purple bloom, and with a deep breath, he stepped into the rushing river of shoppers and approached a young woman with three children, one of whom was screaming loudly.

"This is for you," Josh heard himself say as he held out the flower and folded piece of paper to the woman. She stopped in surprise and slowly held out a hand to take them.

"Thank you," she said.

"Have a wonderful day," Josh responded, going back to where Maisy was waiting before the woman had a chance to read the note. He looked back and saw that the child had stopped screaming because the woman had given her the purple flower.

He smiled at Maisy. "You're right, this is fun. Let's do it

together." Maisy nodded, and they spent the next twenty minutes picking the most miserable, grumpy looking people to be recipients of their bright flowers and positive messages. Then they spent the next hour in a car park, leaving the rest of the positive notes under windscreen wipers, and leaving change by the parking meters, then finally, they bought lunch for a homeless man who was sitting in a doorway, his cardboard sign simply saying 'Hungry and Homeless.'

When all their flowers, notes and money were gone, they headed back to the park. The sunlight was fading, and Josh felt tired but exhilarated. After seeing the smiles on strangers' faces, and tears of gratitude in their eyes, he began to understand what Maisy had meant about small acts of kindness making a big impact.

But it still didn't feel like enough.

"What can we do next?"

Maisy smiled. "I'll have to go home soon, my mum's expecting me for dinner."

"No, I meant on our rampage of kindness. I want to do bigger things."

"I know what you mean. When I see homeless people my heart breaks. I mean, there are more than enough homes for everyone, there is more than enough food, and there's plenty of money. There's just no reason for people to be living on the pavements. That would never happen on our home planet. We would never see our brothers and sisters go without."

Josh nodded. "It really doesn't make sense. So what can we do about it?"

*   *   *

Sherrie watched herself swimming in her mermaid tail on the screen in the editing suite, and though parts of her segment made her want to cringe and hide her face, she was quite proud of what she had achieved in a short amount of time.

"I think we should keep the part where the dolphin nudged

you and made you giggle, I think it's quite funny," Fin commented as he assisted the video editor in tightening up the piece.

Sherrie laughed. "Sure, why not? It makes it more real. Besides, scripts always go out the window when animals and children are involved, right?"

Fin chuckled. "That's what they say."

Sherrie watched in awe as they cut parts, added parts, adjusted the sound, and generally made the piece look incredible. A few hours later, they watched the final cut, and then Fin gave the go ahead for it to be uploaded to their YouTube channel.

"I think it's a very strong piece, you should be proud of it. You're a natural in front of the camera," Fin complemented her as they headed back to their offices.

"Thank you," Sherrie replied, blushing a little. "It feels good, to be bringing people's awareness to these issues on a bigger scale. Though I still plan to meet up with my friend every week to do our beach clean-up."

Fin smiled. "I think that's great. Sometimes, when people feel like they're making big impact, they abandon the little things they used to do, they see them as being unimportant now. But actually, they remain important, and still need to be done."

"I wish my husband felt the same way," Sherrie said. "He doesn't understand why I feel the need to devote my life to this, why I can't just do my job then come home and switch off from it."

"You can't switch off a passion like yours," Fin said. "Though I'm sure you could transfer the passion to another area of your life, maybe that's what he wants."

Sherrie's blush deepened and when they stopped at her office door, she looked down at her hands rather than look up into his amazing blue eyes.

"Sherrie," Fin said.

Sherrie looked up, the tone of his voice intriguing her.

She'd never heard him say her name in that way before.

"Would you like to have a coffee after work to celebrate getting your first video done and released?"

Sherrie's eyes widened. Hadn't she only just mentioned her husband who felt neglected? But then, he was right, they should celebrate. After all, it wasn't like Jim would want to go out for a drink to celebrate with her, he was too busy being annoyed with her for taking the job.

"Sure," she said, surprising herself. "Why not? We should celebrate. I'll come by your office at five?"

He smiled, and Sherrie melted at the sight of the creases at the corner of his eyes.

"Sure, see you then." He headed down the hall to his office and Sherrie sighed. She went inside, knowing that she would get very little done for the next two hours.

Sure enough, when five o'clock rolled around, all she'd managed to do was write one blog post and send a few tweets to publicise the video, which was already gathering views.

She had texted Jim to let him know she would be working late, feeling a slight twinge of guilt at her lie, then she gathered her things, switched off her computer and headed out the door.

She knocked lightly on Fin's door, and he opened it a second later.

"I'm ready," he said, coming out and locking his office behind him. "The others said they'd meet us there."

"Others?" Sherrie echoed, kicking herself for sounding a little put out.

"Yeah, the rest of the team are joining us, of course."

"Of course," Sherrie said, making the effort to sound enthusiastic. She wondered why she felt so disappointed that she wouldn't get to have Fin to herself. It was crazy, she was married after all, and to a man she loved. Why did she want a date with another guy?

She looked sideways at Fin as they walked down the corridor to the elevator, and she sighed inwardly. He really was beautiful. And passionate, and driven to save the lives of sea animals. It was no wonder she was falling in love with him.

The thought nearly made her gasp out loud, but she caught herself just in time. *Falling in love with him?* Her internal voice exclaimed. *Are you crazy? He's your work colleague, nothing more.*

She nodded to herself. Yes. That was right. Just a colleague, nothing more.

She repeated the sentence like a mantra all the way to the coffee shop, where they were greeted with cheers and applause from the team when they arrived.

Within minutes, Sherrie had forgotten her crazy internal monologue and enjoyed chatting to her team about the next project they had in mind to tackle.

And for the rest of the evening, she avoided Fin's gaze at all costs.

Chapter Eleven

"Thank you so much for having us to stay here with you," Julie said to Violet as they watched the kids running around and exploring the garden.

"You are most welcome, Greg and I are so happy you took us up on the offer. It's not easy, what you've done, and to be able to help you during this tough time is the least we can do."

Julie sighed. "I just hope it's the right thing to do. I mean, for the kids." They both looked over to where the three children were playing catch. "They wanted for nothing when I was with Paul, they always had whatever they needed. But now they will have to go without, I fear."

"Remember what I said in the workshop about manifestation?"

Julie thought back to the Twin Flame workshop and nodded.

"Is that really want you want to manifest into your life? That your children will go without?" Violet asked in a teasing tone.

Julie smiled. "You're right. There's absolutely no reason why I cannot provide all that they need."

"Besides, it wouldn't hurt them to not have everything. I'm sure seeing you happy is probably what they want most of all anyway."

"Yes, it's been quite some time since they've seen that."

"Stay until you feel happy again," Violet said, getting up

and stretching. "Would you like a cup of tea?"

"That sounds great, do you need a hand?"

"Nah, it's cool, just keep an eye on the kids around the pond."

Julie nodded and turned her attention back to where her three children were now playing tag.

They seemed to be happy and carefree. They loved the pod, and so far loved being in the middle of the woods. It was just like a fairy-tale adventure to them. Julie smiled wryly, if only her prince could come along on his white horse to rescue her.

"Here."

Julie looked up to see Violet holding out a steaming mug. She accepted the tea with thanks.

"So other than finding happiness again, what's your plan of action?"

"I'm not entirely sure. I mean, I know I need to find some kind of income, and somewhere for the four of us to live. But what kind of job or where we would live are complete unknowns at the moment."

"That's good. Sometimes it's good to be a little bit vague, it gives the Angels room to get creative on your behalf. Perhaps it would be good to state your intentions as – Universe, I would like to manifest the perfect place for me and my family to live, and an income to support us all."

"That sounds simple enough," Julie said. "I will write that down."

"Of course, you can get more specific, with the kind of home you want, and the amount of income you need, but I always think it's good have some room for improvisation. I have given up on planning anything at all. I tend to just ask the Universe and the Angels to send me whatever is for my highest good, whatever it may be."

"That's brave," Julie commented. "What if they send bad stuff because they think it will help you to grow?"

Violet shrugged. "I have already lived through some of the worst times of my existence, and each time, I have evolved and grown, and become more of the person I know I can be, and have revealed more of my true soul. So bad things are not necessarily a bad thing in my book."

"That's a good way to look at things, I guess," Julie said, taking a sip of her hot tea. "Would still be good to manifest an easy life."

Violet chuckled. "You know that's not what we signed up for when we volunteered to come back this time."

"I know. When I read the part about us all volunteering to come back with you, there was a part of me wondering – why? Why did we do that? Why did we intentionally sign up to come back here to this crazy planet? Haven't we all done this too many times before?"

Violet smiled and patted her hand. "My sweet Old Soul, you volunteered to come out of solidarity and friendship. None of you wanted me to come back by myself. And I do appreciate it. It means so much to me, knowing that all my best warriors are here with me, doing what they can each day to take the world into the Global Awakening."

"Mum! I just saw a dragonfly. It was huge! You have to come and see."

Julie smiled at Violet then jumped up to follow Daniel back to the pond. As she crouched down next to her son, waiting for the dragonfly to show itself again, she thought about how lucky she was, really, and that despite what she'd said, she still would have chosen to return.

All she needed to decide now, was what she wished to manifest for her future.

*   *   *

"Would you like peas with that?"

When the man nodded, Josh added them to his plate, then

carefully passed it to him. "Enjoy your meal."

The man nodded again, then shuffled off to a table to eat. Josh turned to serve the next person in line, looking briefly across to where Maisy was serving pudding. She smiled at him, and he grinned back. After their rampage of kindness, they had found a local soup kitchen, and had decided to spend their weekends volunteering there. There was still a nagging voice in Josh's head, saying that it wasn't enough, but until he figured out the bigger picture, it felt like even doing small things was helpful and beneficial.

After the dinner rush at the shelter was over, Josh hung up his apron and washed his hands, then met up with Maisy outside.

She jumped up from the wall when he approached, and held out a package.

"I wanted to give you this earlier, but we were late for our shift, so I thought I should wait."

Josh took the package. "Is it a special day? Should I have got you something?"

Maisy laughed. "No, though I believe every day is special. Open it."

Josh pulled the brown paper off and found a white t-shirt inside, that had a screen-printed design on it. "*I'm on a kindness rampage*," Josh read out loud, smiling at the design. "That's awesome, you made it at college?"

"Yes, I made myself one too, and I thought we could make more if other people want to join us."

Though Josh knew it would be a great idea to encourage others to join them, so that more good deeds could be done, the idea of sharing Maisy with anyone didn't thrill him. "Maybe we should make a website, or a Facebook page," Josh suggested, immediately putting his new t-shirt on over his clothes.

"That's a good idea," Maisy agreed as they started walking through town to the bus stop. "Do you know how to do that?"

Josh shook his head. "No, not really, I'm not into technology."

Maisy laughed. "Good thing I do then, isn't it? Do you want to come back to my house to start it now?"

Josh nodded. "Sure. I'd love to see where you live."

"It's nothing fancy," Maisy warned.

"Considering we both used to live in caves, I'm sure it will be better than that," Josh teased.

Maisy laughed again, and Josh loved the sound of it. He found himself wanting to make her laugh as much as possible.

Once on the bus, they fell into a comfortable silence, and Josh's mind went into its default mode of thinking through all the possibilities of how he could make a bigger difference to the world.

"One day, I really want to meet Violet," Maisy said suddenly, over the noise of the bus engine.

Josh frowned. "Violet?"

"You know, the lady that wrote the book on the Earth Angel Training Academy. I personally think she must actually be an incarnation of Velvet. I found a picture of her, and she looks incredibly familiar."

"I think you could be right. How else would she have known about all the things she wrote? Where does she live?"

"In the woods in Wales. If a workshop or something comes up that looks good, do you want to go?"

"It would depend on how much it cost," Josh said, thinking of the fact that he had spent all of his savings on their many recent acts of kindness.

"It'll be my treat. It's my birthday soon and my parents asked me what I wanted. I said I wanted to meet Violet. They said I could take a friend when I go."

"Wow, that's really generous. You never told me your birthday was coming up."

Maisy shrugged. "It's no big deal."

"You're going to be seventeen?"

"No, eighteen. I took a year off in-between school and

college because I was ill."

Josh felt his heart constrict at her words. "Ill? What was wrong?"

"Doesn't matter, I'm all sorted now, and getting everything back on track again."

Feeling reassured by her confident tone, Josh let the subject go. A few minutes later, they reached Maisy's stop, and hopped off the bus. She reached out to take his hand, and his heart skipped a beat at the warmth of her small hand in his. Though they weren't dating, and were just very close friends, Josh's feelings for her were getting stronger. His hand tightened around hers. Could she be feeling the same way?

She smiled up at him, then led him down an alleyway in-between some houses which cut through to another street. When she released his hand to get her key out of her bag, he missed it desperately. He wondered when he would next get to touch her skin.

They went straight to the kitchen to get drinks and snacks, then went to Maisy's room. Josh found his eyes darting everywhere, trying to take it all in at once. Her room was like an Aladdin's cave, with her art on the walls, and crystals of every colour and shape taking up space on shelves, her desk, and her bedside table. His gaze came to rest on her bookshelf, and he silently read some of the titles, desperate to borrow them, to take in their wisdom.

He looked up to see Maisy watching him from her desk chair in amusement. "You can borrow some books if you want," she said. "I've read them all already."

"Cool, thanks." Josh reached out and pulled one off the shelf about cosmic ordering.

"It's fun, that one. Let me know how you get on with it."

Josh nodded and put it in his rucksack, then he sat on the edge of the bed while Maisy started up her laptop and opened a browser. "Shall we start with a Facebook page? Then if it starts to grow, move onto a full blown website?"

"Sounds good to me," Josh replied. "Can we use your

graphic from the t-shirt as the main picture?"

"Yes, that's a good idea. Shall we encourage people to do their own acts of kindness, or to join our group?"

"If they're local it would be good to join up together," Josh said, even though he wanted to keep Maisy to himself. "But it might reach people all around the world, in which case we can encourage them to create their own groups."

"Good idea," Maisy said, setting to work on the group page. She filled in all the details, then uploaded the image of her t-shirt design. Josh sat back and relaxed a little. He looked around her room again, taking note of small details. Like the fact that she rode horses as a child, and still had some stuffed animals, hidden by the bed.

"You still don't feel like this is enough, do you?"

Josh looked back at Maisy, and realised that she'd stopped typing and had been watching him for a few minutes. He shook his head quickly. "I think this is a great idea."

"But not big enough," Maisy insisted. "I can feel it in your energy. You don't have much enthusiasm or passion for it, your attention is wandering."

Josh blushed. "I'm sorry, I'm easily distracted."

"No you're not," Maisy insisted. "When you're really into a project, there is nothing that can distract you from it. You forget that we've shared lot of classes since September. I've watched you working. You become utterly absorbed in what you're doing and the rest of the world ceases to exist." She came over to the bed and sat next to him. His mind was whirling; she liked to watch him working on projects at college? He'd had no idea.

"You're right, I suppose, I do get wrapped up in my work. And yes, I guess part of me does feel like this isn't enough. I mean, we're just trying to put a bandage on a very big problem. It feels like we're trying to heal the symptoms, not go to the source and heal the cause of the problem."

"You're right, of course. We are just dealing with the minor stuff. After all, feeding a homeless person for one day doesn't get them off the streets. For that to happen, they need help finding work and somewhere to live. I'm sure there are organisations that offer those services."

"So why are there still people living on the pavement then? It doesn't make any sense."

"Okay, so let's focus on that. Let's do some research into the organisations in the UK tackling the problem, let's talk to the people on the streets, let's get to the root of it, and then see if there's anything we can do to solve it."

"You really think we should?"

"Why not? I didn't have any other plans for this summer once the college year finishes, did you?"

Josh shook his head. "Not really. Where do we start?"

Maisy smiled and leaned over to kiss him on the cheek. "Let's start locally, then widen the area of research."

Josh nodded, but he wasn't really listening, all he could think of was her soft lips touching his skin. Why had she just kissed him? Was she flirting with him? He wished that girls came with an instruction manual, it would make being a teenager much easier.

They spent the rest of the afternoon researching organisations that dealt with homeless issues, and decided to write to them to ask what they could do to help, and also how they could address the causes, in order to prevent homelessness before it happened.

"Maybe it would be helpful to interview homeless people and make a list of all the reasons why they have become homeless, then look at the organisations that tackle those issues," Josh suggested, finally moving his thoughts away from how much he wanted to kiss Maisy.

"That's a brilliant idea," Maisy said, typing furiously as she made notes on her laptop. "We can offer the homeless some food in exchange for their story. We could document it all and put it together into a project of some kind. Even if it's just to raise awareness of the issues."

Josh leaned over her shoulder to read her notes on the

screen, and breathed in the scent of her hair. He closed his eyes, his mind now scrambled again.

Chapter Twelve

"You're going where?!"

Sherrie winced as Jim's voice raised an octave, and she quietly repeated herself. "Japan. There's a real issue with them killing sharks out there, and the charity want me to do the piece on it."

"Japan. To save sharks. Are you fucking serious? You couldn't make this shit up!" He slammed his fist on the dining table and Sherrie jumped. He'd been unhappy ever since she'd taken the job, but this was the angriest she'd seen him yet.

"Jim," she said softly. "You know that this is what I've always wanted to do. To really make a difference, to save the sea creatures, to make the oceans cleaner. And I'm doing it. Can you not be happy for me?"

"Happy that you're running away to the other side of the world? Are you crazy?"

Jim stood up suddenly, knocking his chair over. He stormed off to the bedroom and Sherrie sighed. She picked at her salad, her appetite gone. She had been so excited when Fin had told her about the new project, but now the idea just gave her a headache. Maybe she was crazy for agreeing to do it.

"You're not going."

Sherrie turned to see Jim standing in the doorway to the kitchen. "I won't let you go. So you're not going."

Sherrie frowned, and anger began to rise up in her. "Last time I checked, being my husband didn't entitle you to treat me like a child and order me around like you're my father. I don't need your permission to go. Besides, I've already said I would."

"Fine. Go. But take all your stuff, and don't bother to come back."

Sherrie's mouth dropped open and she stared at Jim. "What?"

"If you want to leave so bad, you can leave for good. Pack up all your stuff. You can find somewhere else to live when you get back from the trip."

"Jim?" Sherrie got up and went over to her husband, but he refused to let her touch him. "What's going on? I don't want to break up, I don't want to leave you for good. This is just a work trip, that's all. I'll only be gone three weeks."

"Then you'll be onto the next project in the fucking Antarctic! No, I didn't sign up for a wife that goes off gallivanting around the world. If you want to travel for work, you'll have to find another husband to support you."

Sherrie blinked back tears, but was unable to stop them from falling. "You don't want to be with me anymore?"

"No. I don't."

The tears were coming faster and Sherrie choked back a sob. "I see," she said, her voice cracking. "I'll pack my things then."

"Good."

Jim went to the front door, grabbed his keys and stormed out of the apartment, and Sherrie stared at the door in shock for several seconds before collapsing onto the floor in a heap, tears streaming down her cheeks. How could he do this? She was finally living her mission, finally happy with her work and her life, and he decides he doesn't like it?

Her anger rose back to the surface, and her tears began to subside. He couldn't abide by a globetrotting wife? Well she couldn't abide by having a dream-killing husband.

She picked herself up off the floor, and headed to the bedroom to get her suitcases. She had no idea where she would go, but she knew she couldn't stay there a moment longer.

She dragged the cases off the top of the wardrobes, and opened them up. She threw as many clothes as she could fit in them, then filled a couple of boxes with some books and accessories and jewellery, though she purposely left everything that Jim had ever given her.

Once she was happy she had everything she wanted, she dragged it all out to her car, and shoved it all in the back seat and the trunk. Finally, she went back to the door and locked it, then she pulled her wedding and engagement rings off, and posted them through the letterbox along with her house key.

"Goodbye, Jim," she said, her anger carrying her all the way to her car, and about half a mile down the road. Then she had to pull the car over because her vision was too blurred.

She went into shock and started shaking all over, and she knew that she wouldn't be able to drive anywhere for some time. Without even thinking about it, she got her phone out and called the only person she wanted to speak to in that moment.

"Hey, Sherrie, are you okay?"

The sound of him saying her name started up the tears again, and his tone changed to one of concern. "Sherrie, what's happened? Are you alright? Where are you?"

Sherrie managed to choke out the bare minimum of details, and without a moment's hesitation, Fin told her he would be with her in fifteen minutes.

She hung up the phone, and was overtaken by sobs again. Her heart felt like it had been torn out, shredded up, and then stuffed back into her chest. When Fin arrived, almost precisely fifteen minutes later, the sobs had subsided, but the tears were still flowing. She was a little embarrassed to see that he'd come with his housemate.

"Sherrie," Fin pulled her door open and she got out of the car and collapsed into his arms. He held her tightly while she shuddered.

"What happened?" he asked softly. "Are you hurt?"

Sherrie shook her head. "Jim broke up with me, he told me to leave." She left out the part about the Japanese trip causing the argument.

"Oh, Sherrie, I'm so sorry." Fin guided her around to the passenger side of the car. "Get in, I'll drive you to my place, you can stay with me."

"Oh, I couldn't ask you to do that," Sherrie protested.

"You didn't ask me," Fin said, opening the door and helping her in. "And I insist."

He went back round to the driver's side, and waved to his housemate behind the wheel of his car. They pulled away, and Sherrie dug around in the glovebox for some tissues. She tried to wipe her face but knew that her makeup was probably all over the place and that it was quite pointless really.

"He seriously asked you to leave? Why?"

Sherrie sighed. "He hated my job. He's been angry about it since I took it. When I told him about Japan tonight, he just lost it. Said that he didn't want a wife that travelled the world."

Fin exhaled. "Wow. That's crazy. Surely he knew how happy you are in your job? I mean, this is your dream, isn't it?"

"Yes, it is. And I think that's the problem. I'm living my dream, and he's not living his."

"I guess I can understand that, to an extent. I'm so sorry, Sherrie. I can't believe he asked you to choose between your work and him, that's just harsh."

"Do you think I made the right choice? He stormed out, I packed and left, I didn't even wait for him to return to say goodbye," Sherrie's face crumpled again and she gasped for air as more tears threatened to take over.

Fin reached over to grip her shoulder. "It will all be okay. Just come back with me, stay for a bit, let things settle, you never know, he might calm down and see that he's made a massive mistake."

"I posted my house keys and rings through the letterbox," Sherrie said. "I think he's going to assume I've made my decision, and that's that."

"Oh," Fin said. He was quiet then, as he navigated streets that were unfamiliar to Sherrie.

Neither of them spoke again for the rest of the journey. Soon, they were pulling up in front of a small detached home. Fin parked, then got out of the car, running around to open the door for Sherrie. She got out, unused to the chivalry. She looked over to see his housemate pulling up behind them and parking. He threw the keys to Fin then went inside the house without a word to them.

"Don't mind him, I interrupted his *Crimson Division* marathon and he's a little peeved at me."

"Oh," Sherrie said. She went to get her case out the back of the car, but Fin handed her a small box and shooed her inside.

"I'll get the rest. Let yourself in and get the kettle on. I'll be there now."

Sherrie nodded and followed his instructions. Once she was settled on the sofa with a hot cup of herbal tea in her hands, her anger and sadness subsided and the reality of the situation finally began to sink in.

"My husband no longer wants me," Sherrie said, hearing the words, understanding the words, but not really believing them. "What am I going to do?"

"Live your dreams," Fin said. "Live your dreams."

* * *

"Are you sure there's no one I can call to come and collect you?

Tadhg shook his head for what felt like the tenth time. "No," he snapped at Lily. "There isn't, just call the damn taxi already."

Lily nodded, unaffected by his tone. It appeared she had become used to his attitude during his stay at the hospital. Occasionally, he felt bad for the way he'd treated her, when she had done nothing other than help him to recover from the accident, but he felt as though the permanent cloud over his head had blocked his ability to notice even the brightest of stars that shone on him.

After what felt like an eternity, because he had nothing to do but stare at the wall, Lily returned to his room with a wheelchair to take him downstairs. He used the crutches to get over to the chair, then flopped down into it, wincing as he jarred his stump which was still very painful. They said it would take some time before it healed enough for him to get a prosthetic.

He refused to speak on the short journey to the exit, where Lily presented him to the cab driver, who took his meagre bag of belongings from her before helping him into the car.

Tadhg looked back at the young nurse, but any words of gratitude got stuck in his throat, and he found himself simply nodding.

"Good luck, Tadhg," she said softly.

He closed the door of the taxi quickly, and waited impatiently for the driver to get back in and drive away. He desperately didn't want Lily to see the tears that were streaming down his cheeks.

As they pulled away, he dug in his pocket for a tissue, and blew his nose, then quickly put away the tissue before the taxi driver could notice what he was doing.

"So you were in an accident?" the driver asked.

Tadhg scowled. He hated nosey people, asking questions they had no right to ask. "Something like that," he muttered, turning to look out of the window. He could feel the gaze of the driver on him in the rear-view mirror, but he refused to look back. Thankfully, his tone must have made him realise that Tadhg was not interested in talking.

They spent the rest of the trip in silence, which Tadhg preferred, and he was relieved when they finally pulled up in front of his building.

The taxi driver looked up at it. "I hope there's a lift in

there," he said.

Tadhg frowned. He hadn't actually considered the practicalities of being an amputee living in a flat on the fifth floor.

"Um, no, there isn't," he replied, mentally trying to figure out how he was ever going to be able to leave his home by himself again. "But don't worry, it'll be fine."

"Right," the driver agreed, his uncertainty clear in his tone. He got out and opened the door for Tadhg, who gave him the fare, with a small tip. The driver waited until he'd got around to the pavement, then handed him his belongings.

"Do you want a hand up the stairs?" he asked.

"No, what I really need is a leg," Tadhg said, surprising himself with the sarcastic joke. He didn't do jokes.

The driver laughed a little, then stopped quickly, looking ashamed at his response. "Right, well, good luck."

He turned and got back into his car, leaving Tadhg on the pavement, leaning on his crutches, wondering how he was going to make it.

Slowly, with the speed of a snail, he made it inside the building, then at an excruciatingly slow pace, made it up one step at a time, with the handles of his bag clenched between his teeth and a death grip on the bannister.

By the time he'd got to the third floor, he was close to tears. His hands were throbbing, he was getting a headache from the concentration and his jaw ached.

At the landing of the fourth floor, he lowered himself to the top step and sat there for a while, panting. His right leg was screaming at him. Though he had done a lot of physical therapy in the hospital, nothing had prepared him for this workout.

He took a few deep breaths, then hauled himself back up, and ignoring all of the pain his body was in, he determinedly made it up the last staircase, and down the corridor, until he was finally standing in front of his own door. He took his key out and opened it, nearly falling through as he lost his balance.

He righted himself and stepped in, looking around his home with new eyes. Except for there being a thick layer of dust, it was exactly as he had left it.

He made his way to the kitchen, filled the kettle and switched it on. It seemed they were incapable of making a decent cup of tea in the hospital, and he was desperate for one. He opened the fridge while the kettle boiled and the stench that hit his senses made his nose wrinkle and he gagged. He needed to do some shopping. But how? He slammed the fridge door shut, and pulled his favourite mug out. He poured hot water onto the teabag, and let it stew for a few moments before removing it. He wasn't keen on black tea but there was no way he was putting his nose in the milk bottle to check it. He picked up the cup, then realised that there was no way he could use his crutches and carry a cup of hot tea at the same time to his armchair.

He growled in frustration, and without another thought, found himself launching the cup at the wall, where it shattered, chips of china flying everywhere, and boiling water splashing his skin.

Annoyed that he had just broken his favourite mug, and he still didn't have anything to drink, Tadhg slid down the cupboards until he reached the floor, and feeling utterly defeated, he sobbed.

The sound of his phone ringing pulled him out of his misery, and not having the energy to pull himself up, he ditched his crutches and crawled across the floor, avoiding as much of the jagged china as he could. His stump throbbed as he dragged it across the floor, but he kept going, until he reached the low coffee table where the phone was.

"Yes?"

"Tadhg? Is that you? Why didn't you answer this morning? I've been so worried, are you okay?"

"Oh, hi, Mum."

Chapter Thirteen

"Can I help at all?"

Greg looked up at Julie, who was standing in the doorway of the kitchen looking uncertain. Violet was away doing a workshop, and Greg was making dinner for her and the kids.

He smiled at her. "You could peel and chop if you want, that would be great."

Julie nodded and went over to the counter. Greg handed her a knife and a peeler, and she set to work.

"The kids okay?"

"Yes," Julie replied, chopping the ends off the carrots. "They're watching a movie upstairs. There was a slight argument over what they would watch; your DVD collection really is epic."

Greg chuckled. "That's down to Violet, she's the movie freak. Though there was already a decent collection here when we took over."

"What happened to the previous owners of the retreat?"

Greg didn't answer immediately, and Julie was worried she'd asked an insensitive or inappropriate question.

"I'm sorry," she said, "I didn't mean to pry."

"No, it's fine. I suppose I still find it difficult to talk about, which I hadn't realised until the moment you asked." He sighed and stirred the onions. "The retreat was previously owned by Esmeralda and Mike. They were Incarnated Angels, and they were amazing. About four years ago, Esmeralda became ill with cancer, and within weeks of the diagnosis, she passed away."

Despite not even knowing them, Julie felt tears fill her eyes.

"Then six months after she passed away, Mike, who was utterly devastated from losing her, was in a car accident and he passed over too."

The tears spilled over and Julie wished she were chopping the onions so she had the excuse of why she was crying.

"In their will, they left the retreat to Violet and I," Greg continued. "It was quite a shock to us, but knowing how passionate they were about reuniting the Flames, it certainly made sense."

Julie nodded, still feeling choked up. She wiped her eyes with her sleeve. A thought occurred to her. "Who were they? Did they go to the Academy?"

Greg smiled. "Yes, Violet told me that you were there, that you were the Professor of Patience."

"Yes, when I read her book, I remembered it all, exactly as she described."

"Esmeralda and Mike were the second-year students that Violet wrote about, their names were Emerald and Mica."

Tears filled Julie's eyes again as she recalled not only what was written about them in the book, but also her own memories of the two Angels sat in the Angelic Garden by the waterfall.

"They were beautiful souls," she said.

"They were," Greg agreed. "And to be honest, the only thing that got us through the ordeal of losing them both was that we knew they would be together again."

"Yes, of course they would be."

Greg took the carrots that Julie had peeled and chopped and added them to the pan. She got started on the rest of the vegetables.

"Violet said that you were trying to work out what you wanted to do now."

Julie sighed. "Yes, I still have no idea what I want to do, or where I should be, or how on earth I'm going to provide for my kids."

"Would you like to do an emotional release session?"

Julie stopped chopping for a moment and looked up at Greg. "What is that?"

"Basically it's a session to identify the trapped emotions from your past that are holding you back, then releasing them. You don't have to talk about them or even know what they are to get rid of them, so it's not like therapy or counselling where you have to dig up and talk about all the bad stuff that's happened."

Julie thought about it for a moment. "It sounds good, but I don't want to put you out any more than we already have, I mean taking up a pod, and your food and…"

"Don't be silly. We're happy to have you stay here with us. And Violet wouldn't have it any other way."

"Okay, thank you. When would be good?"

"How about later when the kids are asleep? You'll be able to relax, and also, the session might make you really tired, so it's good if it's just before bedtime."

"Great, thank you." Julie handed him the rest of the vegetables and he added them to the pan, before adding tomatoes and boiling water.

"The soup will take a while to stew, fancy a glass on the patio?" Greg said, holding up a bottle of red wine.

"Sounds perfect to me," Julie replied, washing her hands and drying them. She followed Greg outside, where he poured them both a glass of wine. She relaxed back into the chair.

"I don't know how Violet can bear to be away from this place," she remarked. "It's so relaxing, it makes me want to never leave." She held out a hand. "Don't worry, we will, I don't mean that we're going to squat here forever, I promise."

Greg chuckled. "You're hardly squatting. But I know what you mean. The travelling and the workshops and talks that Violet does can be really tiring and stressful. She's always very pleased to be home afterwards. Sometimes she even sleeps for a whole day when she gets back, just to get herself back on an even keel."

Julie nodded. "I can imagine it's exhausting."

"What is it you love to do?" Greg asked, taking Julie by surprise.

"What do you mean?" she asked.

"What are you passionate about? What makes you want to jump out of bed in the morning?"

"Besides the kids?" When Greg nodded, Julie thought for a moment. She couldn't remember the last time she had voluntarily jumped out of bed in eager anticipation.

"I loved throwing parties," she found herself saying. "Organising, sending the invites, decorating, then of course, the socialising." She laughed. "Even as a child I was always throwing teddy bear picnics and tea parties." She shook her head. "It's been a while since I organised a party. I think the last time was one of the children's birthdays."

Greg nodded. "Could be something you could do professionally."

"What? Have parties?"

"Organising events for other people," Greg said, standing up. "I'd better give it a stir. Shall I do some garlic bread?"

Julie nodded. "That sounds great. I'll set the table, are we eating out here?"

"Why not?" Greg said over his shoulder as he returned to the kitchen.

Julie put bowls and cutlery out on the tables, and twenty minutes later, she ushered the kids downstairs, despite their moaning about wanting to watch the movie. Greg lit some citronella candles to keep the bugs away, and the kids made lively conversation while they ate their dinner.

After some ice cream and much cajoling, all three kids were finally tucked up in their beds in the pod, and Julie put a cardigan on to ward off the evening chill before going back to the house for her session.

"Mummy?"

Julie turned around to see Jerry watching her. She went over to his side. "What is it?" she whispered, trying not to disturb Daniel and Charlotte.

"I miss Daddy," he whispered back.

Julie smiled at her youngest. "I know, baby. I do too, sometimes. It's okay to miss him. It'll just make seeing him again so much more special."

"But when will I see him?"

"Soon," Julie promised. "Mummy needs to decide on a few things first, before we can move forward."

"Okay," Jerry replied with a yawn.

Julie kissed him gently on the forehead. "I love you, sweetheart."

"Love you too, Mummy."

Julie tucked his covers in a little tighter, and his eyes closed. She stood up and left the pod, her eyes stinging a little from unshed tears. She hoped that her session with Greg would help her to gain a little clarity.

Because despite his suggestion, she really had no idea what to do.

* * *

"So are you glad you stayed?"

Helen looked up at Chad, and wiped her hand across her sweaty forehead. She grinned. "I'm sweating like a pig, covered in dust and dirt, every muscle in my body aches and I desperately need to sleep."

"I'll take that as a yes then," Chad teased.

Helen laughed. "Yes, I'm glad I stayed. When I first got here I didn't think I would utter that sentence, but it seems you were right, after all."

"Well, in celebration of me being right, shall we go out for a drink this evening?"

Helen wiped her hands on her grime-covered t-shirt. "A

drink?"

"You know, liquid generally served in a glass that quenches the thirst."

Helen stuck her tongue out at him, making him laugh. "I know what a drink is. It's just I don't really drink alcohol."

"It doesn't have to be alcoholic. I'm sure we can find a decent virgin cocktail or a cup of tea. What do you say?"

Helen shrugged. "Okay. I do need to shower and change first though. What time are you thinking?"

"Shall we say eight? After dinner?"

"Sure, sounds cool." Helen picked up her brush again, and continued sweeping up the dust from the days' building work.

"Cool, see you later." Chad went back to his own part of the building, and Helen smiled. She wasn't sure, but she thought she'd just been asked out on a date. Her smile slipped from her face as she mentally reviewed her wardrobe. She really didn't have anything nice to wear.

She glanced down at her filthy work clothes and shrugged. As long as she was clean, she guessed it didn't really matter.

Impatient to finish, Helen worked more quickly than normal, which meant the sweat was literally dripping from her when she finished. She walked back to the charity headquarters, and dashed up to her room to find something suitable to wear and scrub the grime off her body.

An hour later, finally feeling clean and refreshed, she went down to the dining hall, and found that Chad had saved her a seat next to him at the table.

She sat down and he grinned at her. "Hungry?"

"I'm famished," she replied, accepting a full plate and immediately tucking in.

They didn't talk much during the meal, and Helen was happy to listen to the chatter around them of their fellow volunteers.

"Hey, Helen, think we'll get your section finished up tomorrow?" Ken asked.

Helen looked across the table at the older man. "I don't

see why not," she said with a smile. "As long as you pull your weight of course."

Ken laughed and the others whistled. "I know I'm not as fast as you," Ken said. "But you are a lot younger."

"And a lot prettier, too," added Reuben.

There was more jeering and teasing and Helen blushed. Chad leaned closer to her and whispered in her ear. "You do look very pretty tonight."

Her blush deepened, and Helen continued eating, trying to ignore the butterflies fluttering around in her stomach.

The conversation moved on and Helen was glad to finally get out of the dining hall and out into the cooler evening air.

"Ready?"

Helen looked up to see Chad coming through the door and smiled.

"Yes. Do you have somewhere in mind for tonight's jaunt?"

"I do, actually, it's my favourite little café, and it just so happens it's open until late at night."

Helen fell into step beside him as they made their way down the street, still bustling with activity despite the hour. Helen breathed in deeply, realising that all of the smells and sounds and sights that had overwhelmed her senses when she first arrived there, were now her favourite thing about the foreign city. They kept her in the present moment, because she was so acutely aware of them.

She figured that after some time, she would become used to it and it would all fade a little into the background, but part of her hoped that wouldn't happen.

After walking for ten minutes, Chad led the way into a tiny, ramshackle building. Helen followed him in, and when her eyes adjusted to the oil lamp-lit gloom inside, she looked around and smiled. It was very cosy, and she loved the quirky decor. Chad went up to the counter and ordered two teas. He didn't ask her what she wanted, which partly irritated her, and partly made her feel good.

"Psychic are we?" she commented, her irritation winning over.

Chad frowned. "I don't understand?"

"You didn't even ask me what I wanted to drink, you just ordered for me."

"I'm sorry, that was terribly rude of me, but honestly, you've got to try their tea, it's the best I've found. Besides, I thought Brits were all tea-drinkers?"

Helen shrugged. "True as that may be, I still would like to decide for myself."

Chad held his hands up. "I'm really sorry, I won't do that again. And if you hate the tea, I will gladly get you a different drink, one of your own choosing."

Helen nodded. "Okay."

The lady brought their drinks over then, and Helen went to stir some sugar into her cup but Chad stopped her.

"Trust me, you don't want to do that, try it without sugar first."

Helen's eyebrows shot up. "Really? First you order for me, now you won't let me have sugar?" Her irritation went up a notch and she wondered why she had agreed to come out for the evening.

Chad sat back and shook his head. "I'm sorry. Can we start again? I'm really messing this up right now."

Helen pursed her lips. "Yes, you are." She took a sip of the hot tea, without the sugar, and sighed. He was right. It really did taste great, even without her preferred level of sweetness.

"Okay, so it's good, thank you for the recommendation."

"You're welcome," Chad said cautiously.

There was an awkward silence then, and Helen felt her earlier irritation melt away a little. She knew she was just being a bit bristly because she was tired. She had never done so much physical labour in all her life, and she felt exhausted at the end of every day.

"How long have you been in Nepal?" she asked, to break

the tension in the air. She realised that she knew very little about Chad, they hadn't discussed much besides their project since she'd arrived.

Chad visibly relaxed a little and smiled. "About six months. Decided to take a break from work, and travel for a couple of years. I had enough savings to live off, so I figured I should volunteer my time. I found this charity, and I fell in love with it, so I decided to stay here."

Helen nodded. "How much longer do you plan to stay here for? Don't your family miss you?"

"I'm not sure. My family do miss me like crazy, especially my brother. This is the longest we've ever been apart, and I know it's killing him. But it feels important, to be here, to do this. They understand, but they do ask me every time I call when I'm coming home."

"Where is home?

"Arkansas." Chad smiled. "Not as cool as coming from California or New York, I'm afraid."

"It's cool. Hell, I come from a council estate in England. Arkansas sounds pretty exotic in comparison."

Chad laughed. "I don't think anyone has ever described it as exotic before. My brother will find that amusing."

Helen sipped more of her tea, and found that she was enjoying Chad's company. Her earlier mood had dissolved completely, and she found that she liked looking into his deep blue eyes, and the dimples in his cheeks when he smiled and laughed were really cute.

"So *are* you really glad you stayed?"

Helen smiled. "Yes, I am. I've never been so exhausted in all my life, but I'm loving every moment of it. And to think that families will finally have somewhere to live after living in shelters for the last couple of years, makes me feel like I've actually done something worthwhile."

"I'm sure you've done other worthwhile things in your life."

Helen wrinkled her nose. "Not really. I've worked in

normal jobs, had boring relationships," she shrugged. "My life has been pretty unremarkable really. Which is why things had to change. I knew that if I lived one more day devoid of colour, laughter or emotion, I would rather just not be here."

Helen rubbed the side of her eye to stop a tear, and stared down into her empty tea cup. She couldn't quite believe she had just admitted to a near stranger that she had considered committing suicide.

After a long silence, she snuck a glance up at his face, and he was watching her intently. She waited for him to speak.

"I get you," he said softly. "I was in the same space. I couldn't face going to work and sitting in an office cubicle anymore. It felt like I wasn't living, I was merely existing, earning a wage to pay rent and bills, and going through the same shit every day."

Helen nodded. She was glad that he understood and wasn't judging her.

He reached across the table to touch her hand and a little tingle went through her. "I'm glad you chose to travel instead," he said.

She smiled. "I'm glad you did, too."

Chapter Fourteen

"Thank you so much for letting me stay here," Sherrie said, as Fin handed her a mug of coffee.

"You're completely welcome. Couldn't have the star of our show living on the streets," Fin teased.

"I would hope it wouldn't have come to that. Though I didn't foresee him emptying the joint account." She shook her head and sipped her drink. "I knew that account was a bad idea, I had a feeling I should keep some personal accounts too."

Fin shrugged. "It's easy to see in hindsight, don't knock yourself, you had no idea any of this was going to happen."

"True."

They sat down at the breakfast bar to eat their cereal. "It just seems a little crazy that my husband broke up our marriage over a work trip, and now that trip has been cancelled."

Fin waved his spoon at her. "Perhaps that was the entire function for the trip though, to help you to see your relationship for what it was. And now you have, the function of the trip has been realised and no longer needs to actually happen."

"Or perhaps it's just that we don't have enough funding to go to Japan," Sherrie said sarcastically in between mouthfuls of muesli.

"Yeah, that too." Fin sighed. "I get so frustrated sometimes, when there are causes that need to be made public so they can be resolved, yet there isn't enough money for us to do that. I mean, soon, sharks will be an endangered species, yet it won't be until they're extinct that someone will say – gee, we really should have done something about that."

Sherrie listened to Fin's passionate rant and found herself wanting to kiss him. She shook her head. "I know, I always felt like it would actually take the end of the world for people to finally realise that we should have been doing something to prevent the disasters all along."

"If the world was to end tomorrow, what would you do today?"

Sherrie frowned. Though his tone was teasing, his eyes were very serious as he waited for her answer. "Is there anything I can do to prevent this hypothetical end?"

"No, it'll end tomorrow, regardless of what you choose to do today."

"Okay, in that case, I suppose I would go to the beach with someone I loved, eat ice cream, swim, sunbathe, and read a book."

Fin picked up his bowl and mug and took it to the sink. He set it down then turned back to her. "Let's do it. Let's live today as though the world were ending tomorrow."

Sherrie laughed. "Are you serious? We have work today, deadlines that need to be met, remember?"

"Screw them. Let's have fun."

Sherrie picked up her own bowl and mug and went to the sink to rinse it out. She thought about it for a few moments, then shrugged. "Why not?" she said. "They can hardly fire us both."

"Awesome. Go get your bathing suit, and we'll get out of here. I'll grab my surf board." He grinned and reached out to squeeze her arm. "I'll text the boss to say we're both ill with a bug. They know you're crashing here, so it should work."

Sherrie giggled and went to the spare room to get changed. She put on a bikini and shorts and a t-shirt, then threw some suntan lotion, a book she'd been trying to read for months, a towel, and some money into a small knapsack.

Within fifteen minutes, they were in Fin's car, making their way to the coast. The Californian sunshine shone down on them, and Sherrie enjoyed the breeze rippling through her tangled red hair.

"I'll get the ticket," Fin said when they'd parked up. She nodded and he ran over to the machine. They then made their way over the dunes to the beach, Fin carried his board under one arm.

Being a weekday, the beach was pretty much deserted. Sherrie set her knapsack down, and decided to head straight to the water before sunbathing and reading her book. She took off her sunglasses and shrugged off her shorts and pulled off her shirt.

"Race you!" she yelled over her shoulder, as she ran across the sand.

"Hey!" Fin yelled back, as he dropped the board on the sand and quickly pulled off his clothes before running after her. They hit the surf and Sherrie yelped as the cool water hit her warm bare skin.

She waded in further, then screamed again when an arm wrapped around her middle and picked her up. Fin swung her around then set her down in the water, and in response she kicked her foot and splashed him.

"Oh, like that is it?" he said, kicking water back at her.

She giggled and waded in further, and they messed about in the surf until they were both drenched. Sherrie then dove into the deeper water and swam a bit further out. She looked back to see Fin leaving the water and running across the sand to get his board. She swam further still, then floated on her back, allowing the waves to push and pull her as they pleased. The waves weren't very big, but she supposed Fin might catch one or two good ones.

"Hey, don't go too far out."

Sherrie righted herself in the water and saw Fin paddling

out to her, and she realised she was quite far from the shore. She swam back toward him, then just to freak him out, she dove into the water and swam underwater for a few metres. She could see his board up ahead, and she popped up out of the water just next to him.

"You're crazy," he said, when he saw her.

She rubbed her eyes and pulled her hair out of her face and laughed. "No, I'm a mermaid," she said.

"Yes, you are," he agreed.

Sherrie treaded water next to his board for a few seconds, and became aware that he was staring into her eyes quite intensely. Seeing as they were living the day as though it were their last, she figured she had nothing to lose, so she leaned forward and acted upon her impulse from that morning.

When her salty lips met his, she felt warmth, but nothing else.

After a moment, she pulled away and they looked into each other's eyes.

"I think it's too soon," Fin said gently.

Sherrie bit her lip and nodded. "You're right. I'm sorry."

"Please, don't ever apologise for kissing me. I'm just sorry that it's not the right time right now."

"Me too." Sherrie shivered. "I think I'll go sunbathe while you catch some waves."

Fin nodded and she swam back to shore. She reached the sand and stood up, readjusting her bikini as the water pulled it downwards. She got back to her knapsack and pulled out her towel. After a quick rubdown, she lay it on the sand and settled on it to watch her friend surf.

Though part of her had been hoping for sparks, there was another part of her that had known it wouldn't be right. It was a little like kissing her brother.

She sighed and picked up her book, turning to the dog-eared page. She stared at the words, but had no idea of their meaning.

* * *

"What the hell are you doing here?"

Lily grinned and gently pushed past Tadhg and walked into his flat. She went straight to the kitchen and set down the bags she was carrying on the counter.

"Nice to see you too," she called over her shoulder, to where Tadhg still stood, leaning against his door frame, feeling a bit shocked.

"How did you even get into the building?"

"Oh," Lily said, waving her hand. "A lovely guy from the floor below you was coming in at the same time and let me in. I figured you might be struggling a little with cooking and whatever, so I came to check on you."

Tadhg scowled. "I wish you'd let me know you were coming." He looked around the flat, which was in complete disarray, as he hadn't bothered to pick up after himself or clean for several days.

"So you could tell me to fuck off and leave you alone?" Lily asked with a laugh. She turned around and grinned at him, a packet of cheese in her hand.

Shocked at her language, Tadhg could only nod in response, making her laugh again.

She went to the fridge, opened the door then stepped back quickly and slammed it shut again. "Holy shit, what the hell died in there?" she exclaimed. "Even the morgue doesn't smell that bad."

Feeling thoroughly offended, even though he had to agree with her – the smell was shockingly bad – Tadhg opened the front door. "Maybe you should just go, I can take care of myself, thank you."

She raised her eyebrows at him. "Yeah, I can see that. Look, why don't you just sit down and chill." She rolled up her sleeves. "I'll get this under control in a jiffy. Would you like a cuppa?"

Defeated by her tone of voice, he sighed and slammed the

front door, then made his way across to his favourite armchair, before flopping into it.

The TV switched on and he realised he must have sat on the remote.

"Any amazingly depressing stuff on the news at the moment?" Lily asked as he heard her clattering about in the kitchen.

He rolled his eyes. "Same old, same old. The government is determined to send the whole country down shit creek without a paddle."

He heard a giggle, which irritated him further. A few minutes later, Lily appeared with a cup of tea for him. With milk in it.

"Thank you," he said begrudgingly, accepting the hot mug.

"You're welcome," Lily sang. She went back to the kitchen, and Tadhg tried to relax back into his chair and enjoy his cup of tea, but the idea of some crazy woman messing with stuff in his kitchen didn't make him feel very relaxed.

After not watching the news for what felt like forever but was probably about thirty minutes, Lily finally came back into the lounge, and she tidied it up, throwing all the rubbish from his many takeaways into a black bag.

"Planning on living on pizza and Chinese for the rest of your life?" she remarked.

"Why not?" he said. "No prep, no cooking time, no washing up."

"With the added bonus of never having to open your fridge again," she said, a smile on her face.

"Yeah, exactly."

Once the room was in order, Lily piled up two black bags by the door, then she went and made herself a cup of tea and then flopped onto the sofa.

"I can't stay long, I have a shift later."

"I didn't ask you to waste your time off trying to look after me."

She looked at him sideways. "No, you didn't. I came over because you were the grumpiest, most miserable patient I've had in a long time, and you had no visitors, so I figured that you would be all on your own, trying to figure out how to live with just one leg. Have you looked at the information we gave you on claiming benefits?"

"I'm the grumpiest patient you've ever had? Why on earth would you care about helping me then?"

Lily shrugged. "I figured that something really shitty must have happened for you to get that grumpy, and I felt bad for you."

Tadhg frowned. "I don't need anyone's pity."

Lily shook her head. "No, but you could do with a bucketful of love."

Tears filled Tadhg's eyes suddenly, and he blinked rapidly, trying to keep them back, but it was too late. The word love had triggered something deep inside him.

Of course, Lily was too observant to miss the tears trickling down his cheeks, even though he quickly looked away.

"You deserve to be loved," Lily said softly, reaching out to pat his hand. "Even if you have caused near fatal accidents and are a grumpy old git."

Tadhg chuckled through his tears and nodded. What was she doing to him? How did she have the power to reduce him to a watery mess?

The phone interrupted his internal musings and his eyes widened in horror. "Don't pick that up," he said. But it was too late. The young nurse was too quick. She pounced on the phone and answered it, no doubt curious to see who would be calling the grumpiest man alive.

"Tadhg's phone," she answered chirpily. "Sure he's here, can I ask who's calling?"

Tadhg saw her eyes widen and he groaned. His mother always had impeccable timing.

"You're his mum? But where were you?"

Tadhg groaned louder and held his hand out. "Give that to me," he hissed.

Lily shook her head. "Where were you when Tadhg was in hospital? He was with us for weeks, and he didn't have a single visitor. I assumed he had no family or friends."

Tadhg dropped his head into his hands. The cat was well and truly out of the bag now.

"He was in an accident. Didn't you know about it? Oh my goodness, that's crazy. I'm so sorry you weren't informed, we didn't have your details. You weren't listed as next of kin."

Tadhg listened to Lily's half of the exchange in horror. He looked up and waved his arms madly to get her attention. He pointed to his stump and then shook his head frantically.

"Yes, he was very badly injured. They had to amputate his left leg." Lily paused. "No, this isn't a joke, I'm the nurse who was caring for him."

"Give me the phone," Tadhg barked, losing his temper completely.

Lily finally handed the phone over, and then sat down and continued to drink her tea.

Tadhg carefully put the phone to his ear, only to be barraged by his mother's sobbing and gabbling.

"Mum, it's okay, she didn't mean it, I'm fine really, it was only a minor accident. Mum, please calm down, shhh, I'm fine." He sighed. She was blubbering incoherently now. Suddenly, another voice came over the line.

"I'm so sorry, Jemma, Mum's just had some bad news, could you calm her down and reassure her that I'm fine? Yes, I'm sure she will be fine by tomorrow. Thank you, okay bye."

Tadhg clicked the red button then glowered at Lily.

"Just what, in the hell, did you think you were doing?" he said, his teeth gritted together.

"She deserved to know. Poor woman had no idea her son had just lost his leg!"

"That poor woman, my mother, barely even knows she still has a son, which is why she is not my next of kin. She has dementia, and your only saving grace right now is that her short-term memory is so bad that she won't remember your conversation with her by tomorrow."

Lily's eyes were as wide as saucers. "Shit. I'm so sorry. I shouldn't have meddled. It's a weakness of mine, I stick my nose where I'm not supposed to. Will she be okay?"

Tadhg sighed. "Yes, she will be. But I want you to leave now."

Lily nodded and took her cup and his back to the kitchen. Tadhg hated that she had tears in her eyes, and he hated even more that it bothered him.

She came back into the room, but refused to look him in the eye. "There's some ready meals in the fridge, which I've cleaned out. You just need to pop them in the oven. I think they'll be nicer than the takeaways." She looked up then, and her tears spilled over. "I'm sorry for upsetting you and your mum. I just wanted to help."

"It's okay," Tadhg said, surprising himself.

Lily nodded but looked unconvinced. She went to the door and picked up the rubbish bags, then let herself out.

When the door closed behind her, he wanted to call out for her to come back, to not leave him there. Crazy or not, she did bring a little light to his otherwise dark existence.

But of course he sat there and said and did nothing. He looked around the tidy flat, his gaze resting back on the screen where the news channel was still playing. He pulled the remote out and switched it off. The silence was deafening, and his loneliness was complete.

Chapter Fifteen

"Run that by me again, you're doing what?"

Josh grinned at his mum. "Maisy and I are going to see what it's like to be homeless, and we're going to sleep on the streets for a night."

His mother blinked a few times, taking her time to respond. "Why, exactly, do you want to know what it's like to be homeless?"

Josh shrugged. "We've been volunteering at the soup kitchen, and we've been researching what causes homelessness and what we can do to help people in that situation, but we realised that until you actually walk in someone's shoes, it's difficult to really understand how you can help them."

Josh's mum smiled and reached out to hug him. "You're so thoughtful, so generous. But I really don't think I like the sound of you spending the night out on the streets, just you and Maisy. You're so young, anything could happen to you."

"There are children on the streets. Anything could happen to them too. We're going to fundraise as well, and the money we raise will go to the soup kitchen." He stepped back. "Besides, it's warm, and we'll look after each other."

"I'm still not convinced. How do Maisy's parents feel about it?"

"They gave her permission," Josh said, even though he knew that Maisy had spent quite a lot of time convincing them to let her do it. "They're really proud of her for wanting to change things."

"I'm proud of you too, I just worry about you, that's all."

"I know," Josh leaned forward and kissed his mum on the cheek. "But we'll be fine, I promise. I need to go get our fundraising page set up. Love you." Josh grabbed his drink and snack and retreated to his room, before his mum could say anything further about their plans.

Once his door was closed, he went straight to his computer and switched it on. Maisy was waiting on Facebook for him.

"Hey," he typed. "We're all set. Mum's not impressed but she didn't say no."

"Great," Maisy replied. "Here's the link to the fundraising page, start sharing!"

Josh copied the link and posted it to his timeline, as well as sending it to a few of his friends from school. He was excited about their experiment, partly because he actually wanted to understand what it was like to sleep on the streets, but mostly because he wanted to spend more time with Maisy.

"Let's fundraise for two weeks, then do it," Maisy messaged. "Should be warmer at night then."

"Sounds like a plan," Josh replied. "Still up for the soup kitchen tomorrow? Shall we tell them what we're doing?"

"Yes, I think they'll be quite excited about it. It might even inspire the other volunteers to fundraise too."

"Okay. Hey, did you watch *Crimson Division* last night?"

Josh smiled as Maisy launched into a rant about what had happened in the episode. He didn't even like the TV show, but he knew she loved it.

And he was pretty sure he was in love with her.

* * *

Helen wasn't sure how it had happened, but since their semi-disastrous first 'date', she and Chad had become closer and closer, until one evening, they ended up in Helen's room, kissing.

"Let's take it slow," she whispered as he started to unbutton her top.

"Okay," he replied, moving his hands back to her waist and resuming his kisses.

When they finally came up for air later on, Helen's mind was whirling. In all her plans to travel and to volunteer, she hadn't imagined this happening. She remembered her conversation with Maggie before she left, when she said she had no expectations of meeting her Flame.

She looked into Chad's eyes and wondered if he was her Twin Flame. Though she found him attractive, and enjoyed his company, she didn't feel that intense, deep, ground-shaking connection that she'd read about or heard about. But perhaps it was too early to know.

"I should probably go," Chad said, breaking the silence. "Early morning tomorrow."

Helen nodded. They got up and went to her door. "I'll see you in the morning," Helen said, reaching up to kiss him goodnight.

"Sleep well," Chad replied with a smile as he left, closing the door behind him.

Helen went back to her bed and fell onto it with a sigh. She wished she had a female friend there to talk to, but all of the other volunteers were male. There had been a female volunteer called Aria, but she had only stayed for a week. Helen suddenly sat up and smiled. Maggie had insisted that she write to her whenever she could, so perhaps she needed to pen a letter and ask her friend's advice that way.

She dug out some paper and a pen from her bedside table, and then grabbed the novel she was reading to lean on. She put her nib to the paper and the words were soon flying out. She realised just how much she had been holding inside since she'd arrived in Nepal, and a couple of times, the words became blurry as her eyes filled with tears.

By the time she signed her name at the bottom and put it

in an envelope with her friend's name and address on it, she felt so much better. She knew that Maggie would have the perfect advice for her. When she put her book and pen away, her gaze fell on a tiny triangle of card sticking out from the back pages. She flicked through and found the business card of the guy she'd met at the airport. She reopened the envelope carefully and added a PS to her letter, asking Maggie if he'd called her for a reading yet. Then she resealed it and decided to mail it the next day when she got a break.

She settled down under the sheets and switched off her light.

"Bring me beautiful dreams, Angels," she whispered, before closing her eyes.

"Helen?"

Helen turned around and her eyes widened in shock. "Mum? What's going on? How are you here?"

Her mother smiled and reached out to her, engulfing her in a hug. She breathed in a cloud of her mother's perfume, and was instantly transported back to when she was seven years old and had last hugged her rose-scented mother.

"I'm here to let you know that things are going to be quite difficult for a little while, but that you will be okay, I promise."

Helen pulled away a little so she could see her mum's face. "What do you mean, things will be difficult? How is this possible, is this a dream? Why have you never visited before?"

"Well, your Guardian Angel came and asked me to visit, you've never needed it before now."

"Never needed it?" Even though Helen knew she was dreaming, tears filled her eyes and spilled down her cheeks. "Mum, I have missed you every single day since the day you died. I thought you were going to come back," her voice cracked. "I waited every day for you to come back, but you didn't."

Her mother engulfed her in another hug and she sobbed in her soft embrace. "Shhh," her mum whispered. "I'm here, I've always been with you, but there were things I needed to do too.

So much change is coming to the world, and you will be a big part of it. So I want you to promise me that no matter how tough things get, you will keep going, you will hang in there. Do you promise?"

"Yes," Helen said into her soft shoulder. "I promise. But what's going to happen? Is it really that bad?"

"I can't tell you. But remember, no matter what, you're never alone, okay?"

"Okay. I love you."

"Love you too, sweetheart. I love you too."

Her mother pulled away and stepped back, but Helen grabbed her hand before she could leave. "Wait, what do you think I should do about Chad, should I be with him? Is he the one?"

Her mother smiled. "I think you should seize the day and enjoy yourself."

Helen frowned, but let go of her arm. The response didn't really answer her question, but before she could ask again, her mother was gone.

Helen's eyes flew open and she gasped and sat up. She had just seen her mother for the first time in twenty years. She flicked on the light and grabbed her pen and wrote down as much of the dream as she could.

"Seize the day," she whispered to herself with a smile. Her mum was right. She should do just that.

Chapter Sixteen

"Julie, I'd like to introduce you to my friend, Tim."

Julie looked up from her laptop and saw Violet walking up to the bench where she sat outside the pod. She placed the computer aside and stood up, holding her hand out to the tall man next to the Old Soul.

"Nice to meet you, Tim, I'm Julie."

He shook her hand firmly, but Julie couldn't help but see a deep sorrow in his eyes, a sadness in his polite smile.

"Good to meet you, Julie. Violet tells me that you remember being at the Academy too."

Julie smiled. "Yes, I was a professor there." She chuckled. "It still feels very bizarre to talk about it, I keep wondering if I'll get locked up for talking about my life in the Fifth Dimension."

Violet laughed too. "In that case, we all need to be locked up. I'm going to put the kettle on, shall we all have some tea and cake on the patio? Unless we're disturbing something important?"

"Tea and cake sounds great," Julie said. "I was just job hunting, I'm sure it can wait." She closed her laptop and put it inside the pod, then followed Tim and Violet back to the house. The kids were with their dad for the weekend, and it felt great to have some peaceful time to herself.

They all sat down at the table and Julie smiled at Tim. "So have you come for the day or are you staying for a bit?"

"I'll be here for a couple of days. I've booked in for some healing with Greg, and then Violet mentioned you were here, and that perhaps we could do some kind of meditation together?"

"Hope that was okay," Violet said as she brought out three huge slices of carrot cake.

"Of course," Julie said, receiving her plate with a smile. "It sounds like a great idea. What is the intention for the meditation? Are you looking for your Twin Flame?"

There was an awkward silence and Violet and Tim looked at each other. Julie saw the pain wash over his face and her heart dropped.

"Something like that," he said softly. "My Twin Flame is on the Other Side. And I would very much like to see if I could contact her through meditation."

"Oh, Tim, I'm so sorry. I had no idea. When did she go home?"

"Eighteen months ago," Tim said, staring down at the table. He shook his head. "It still seems completely unreal. She was in an accident, which paralysed her, but then she passed away almost a year later when she mixed her medication with alcohol and reacted badly to it."

Julie's eyes widened and she reached across to rest her hand on his knee.

"Oh, beautiful Earth Angel, I'm so sorry. That must have been so difficult for you."

Tim nodded. "I just miss her so much. I need to hear from her, know that she's okay. But I've not received any messages from her yet." He pulled his wallet out and showed Julie the photograph of Hannah he had tucked in there.

"She's beautiful," Julie said, looking into the eyes of his Flame.

"She is beautiful, and I have no doubt that she is okay," Violet said, bringing three mugs of tea out. "She was a tough cookie, Hannah. She was an Indigo Child. I'm sure she is just busy on a mission in the Fifth Dimension." She sighed.

"There's also the possibility that she may have gone home to her planet. In which case, it may well be impossible to contact her. But I did promise that we would try."

Tim nodded. "I understand that. And if that's the case, then I will just have to find a way to accept that and move on."

He picked up his mug and took a tiny sip of the hot drink, and Julie's heart ached for him.

"So do you remember Tim?" Violet asked her, as she settled down in her chair.

Julie frowned. "Should I?"

"He was the first trainee to be called to Earth from the last class at the Academy."

Julie's eyes widened and she looked back to Tim, who was taking a bite of carrot cake. The story from Violet's book, and her own memories of the Academy flashed through her mind and she gasped. "Tm! You're the Starperson from Zubenelgenubi!"

Tim smiled. "The one and the same. Violet told me you are Cotton. The Professor of Patience."

Julie nodded. "Yes, it seems to be something I'm having the opportunity to practice a lot in this life."

Tim chuckled. "It feels like that for us all, I think."

"Amen to that," Violet agreed.

The three of them fell silent as they tucked into the cake, and Julie tilted her head back in the sun, enjoying the warmth of the rays on her face.

"Hey, I hope you left some for me."

Julie opened her eyes to see Greg walking up the path, looking grubby and a bit dishevelled.

Tim stood up to greet him and they hugged.

"How's it going?" he asked the Starperson in a low voice. Tim shrugged in reply.

Greg nodded and reached over to nab the last bite of Violet's cake from her plate.

"Oi! There's more in the kitchen. I was enjoying that."

Greg grinned and kissed her on the cheek. "Love you."

Violet shook her head and laughed, and Greg went into the kitchen to get himself some cake.

Julie watched the exchange with a feeling of hope in her heart that one day she might get to experience the kind of connection Violet and Greg had.

Greg reappeared with his cake, and he sat with them while he practically inhaled it.

"Busy day?" Julie asked. She knew he'd gone to do some work on a house nearby. The retreats and Violet's workshops brought in more than enough money to sustain them, but Greg often still enjoyed doing odd jobs locally.

"Yeah, it's getting there though. Another couple of days' work left, I reckon."

"We're going to the meditation tent in a minute, are you going to join us?" Violet asked Greg, gathering up the mugs.

He shook his head. "I'm going to get cleaned up then clear myself and relax, so Tim and I can do a healing session later if that's okay."

Violet nodded and took the mugs back into the kitchen.

"I appreciate you fitting me in," Tim said. "I know you're really busy at the moment."

Greg shook his head. "It's no problem. I need to do more sound healing really, and less manual stuff."

"I really enjoyed my session," Julie said. "It felt like you shifted a lot of the fears I've been carrying around for so long."

Greg smiled. "That's good. Would you write a testimonial?" he asked, half joking.

"Of course," Julie said. "I didn't even think about that. I will write one for you tomorrow."

A seed of an idea was planted in her mind in that moment, and Julie nodded, partly to Greg and to herself. She needed to do some research later.

Violet returned and clapped her hands. "Shall we?"

They headed for the meditation tent, and took their shoes off in the little entranceway before stepping into the white clouds of fabric.

A feeling of peace stole over Julie the moment she stepped in, making her smile. She was intrigued to see what would happen during the meditation.

Once they were settled on their cushions, Violet instructed them to take three deep, slow breaths.

"The meditation I'm going to lead you on is a slightly different version to the one we do during our retreats, with the intention being that when we step through the door, we will enter the space where our Twin Flame is right now, rather than into a past moment where we were with our Flames."

Julie nodded. Having not attended a Twin Flame retreat before, she wasn't entirely sure what to expect, but she figured it didn't really matter. She closed her eyes, and Violet's soft voice took her on a journey that ended up in a hallway with many doors in front of her. She looked closely and saw that the door in front of her bore a golden nameplate that said:

Prof. Blue Cotton. Patience 1000000001.

She grinned and reached out to open the door, but found that when her hand touched the handle, the door disappeared.

She stepped in, and found herself walking down a path to the pebbled shoreline of a still lake. The scene looked too otherworldly to be somewhere on Earth. But perhaps it was just in a different country. She walked down to the edge of the lake, and picked up a pebble to skim on the still water.

"Blue."

She turned, mid throw, and when she saw the figure, she dropped the pebble.

"Who are you?" Julie asked.

The man with huge feathered wings reached her side and smiled.

"I am Aragonite." He reached out to touch her face, and when his fingers made contact with her cheek it was as though she had been electrified. "I am your Flame," he whispered.

Tears came to her eyes and she nodded.

"Yes," she agreed. She looked up into his golden brown eyes and frowned. "You're still an Angel? You have chosen not to incarnate on Earth?"

"I had planned to come to Earth. When you were at the Academy teaching, I was in the higher realms, and I did request to become human so that we could be together again, as we were so many civilisations ago."

"But?" Julie asked.

"But then they were asking for volunteers to go to another Universe. It seems as though Angels are needed to help another planet, much like Earth, that may also be spinning out of control. We won't know the full details until we get there, but I have volunteered my services. Our preparations for the mission are finally complete, and it is now time for us to go."

The tears gathered in Julie's eyes began to fall, and she shook her head. "Can I not go with you? I will volunteer, surely they will need Old Souls too?"

"Only Angels are being called to go," he said sadly. "I'm sorry, my sweet, sweet Blue. I had dreamed of our final lifetime together for some time."

"I only taught patience at the Academy because I needed so much of it myself," Julie confessed. "I felt so impatient inside, wanting so much to be with you, but knowing that it would be a long time." Her voice broke. "But knowing it will never be? I think that's worse than waiting."

"Perhaps I shouldn't have come," Aragonite whispered. "But I selfishly needed to see you." He leaned down and kissed her softly on the lips, and she melted into his embrace. He wrapped his arms around her, and then his giant wings wrapped around them both.

Too soon, he released her and stared into her eyes. "I love you, Blue," he said, tears running down his cheeks. "And even though we will be in different Universes, we will still be connected, we always have been, always will be. Distance and time are irrelevant when it comes to our connection."

Julie nodded, but her heart was breaking. "What will I do now?"

"You will fulfil the mission you set out to do on Earth.

You will assist Velvet with the Awakening, and you will love, laugh, and be happy."

Julie shook her head, the tears coming faster. "I don't feel as though happiness is something I will ever feel again."

Aragonite pulled her in for another kiss. "You will," he promised. "I have no doubt that you will have a happy life."

"Will I ever see you again?"

Aragonite shook his head. "No, this will be the last time."

He stepped back, and his wings rose up as he prepared to fly away.

"No," Julie protested. "Please don't leave me."

"Goodbye, sweet Blue. I love you."

"I love you too," Julie said, clutching her chest. With a single, powerful beat of his wings, he rose up from the pebbled shore, and she watched as he flew away across the lake. The moment after she lost sight of him, she heard a soft voice.

"If you could make your way to your door, we will begin our journey back."

Violet's voice surrounded her, and before she could completely lose it, Julie followed her instructions and returned to the corridor through her door. The moment before she stepped through, she looked back to the lake, where a low mist had begun to roll in.

"Goodbye, Aragonite."

Back in the corridor, she bowed her head. The idea of never seeing her Flame again, of not having their final life together, was crushing her heart. She followed Violet's voice, and moments later, opened her eyes to see Violet and Tim looking at her in concern.

"Julie," Violet said softly. "Are you okay?"

Julie shook her head then dissolved into sobs. Violet came over to her and wrapped her arms around her, holding her while she grieved.

It was a while before she felt calm enough to speak. Violet had led her back to the house, and Tim was making them tea.

"What happened?" Violet asked gently.

Julie described her vision to them, finding it difficult to speak at times.

"Oh, Julie," Violet whispered, pulling her into another hug. "I'm so sorry. But it sounds as though he's an incredible soul."

Julie nodded. "He was magnificent." She accepted the cup of tea from Tim and then looked up at his face. "What happened in your vision, Tim? Did you find Hannah?"

Tim shook his head. "No, there was nothing but white mist when I stepped through the door. I couldn't find her."

Julie's heart hurt for him, he looked as forlorn as she felt. She set her cup down and got up to hug him. "I'm so sorry, I had hoped you would find her."

Tim nodded into her shoulder. "Me too. But I guess I'm just not meant to see her again."

Julie remembered Aragonite's words. "Distance and time between Flames has no relevance. We are connected to them always, no matter where we are."

"Thank you," Tim whispered.

*   *   *

"Hello?"

"Have you forgiven me yet?"

Tadhg frowned at the phone receiver. It seemed as though the crazy nurse refused to give up. "No," he said.

"Okay, I'll try again in a week," she replied cheerfully.

Tadhg sighed. "You're not going to give up, are you?"

"Nope."

"Why?" he asked. "You said yourself I'm a miserable bastard, why not just leave me to sort myself out?"

"Because for the first time in your life, you actually need help, and you don't know how to ask for it or accept it when it's offered. So I feel duty-bound to make sure you get help."

"Duty? You mean you're not just doing this out of pity?" Tadhg asked sarcastically.

"Not just duty," she said. "I like you, Tadhg. I think underneath that tough, crusty exterior, there's a very sweet soul hiding."

"I wish that were true, Lily. But I'm afraid I'm really just miserable to the core."

Lily laughed. "I don't think that's possible. Shall I come over when my shift ends at four? I can go to my favourite deli and get us both dinner."

"Whatever," Tadhg said.

"Excellent, I'll see you then."

Tadhg hung up the phone, and stared at it for a while, ignoring the news still playing on the TV. Why was she so persistent? Though he had forgiven her for upsetting his mum (she was back to normal the next day) he had assumed that she would just back off and leave him alone. Clearly, he had assumed wrong.

He switched off the TV, and looked at the clock. He had three hours before she was going to turn up on his doorstep, so he figured he ought to clean himself up a bit. He had taken to living in his dressing gown and pants, seeing it a pointless waste of time to get clothes dirty when he wasn't leaving the house. At least he had some food in the cupboards, he had actually done some internet shopping for the first time in his life.

He made his way slowly to the bedroom and dug out some clothes from the wardrobe. Then he made his way to the shower, and washed several days' worth of grime from his body.

Feeling fresh and clean, he tended to his stump, which was healing quite well now, then he put the clean clothes on, feeling more human that he had in a while. He caught sight of himself in the mirror and frowned. He looked far too dressed up. She was going to think he had done it for her benefit. He pulled the shirt off, and found a more casual t-shirt instead. He didn't want her to get the wrong impression.

He paused for a moment, as the thought of her getting the

wrong impression lit him up inside. Surely the beautiful young nurse wouldn't be interested in him anyway? After all, he had to be at least ten years older, and he was a cripple.

Shaking his head at himself, he made his way back to the lounge and painstakingly gathered up rubbish that had accumulated since her last visit.

By the time he'd finished and put the kettle on for tea, he was exhausted. He perched on a stool and drank his cuppa next to the kettle, as he still hadn't worked out how to transport a hot drink to his chair without spilling it all.

At quarter past four, he was dozing in his armchair when he heard a voice.

"Tadhg?"

He looked up to see Lily standing in the doorway. He'd left the door open so he wouldn't have to get up to answer it.

"Come in," he said, trying to sound welcoming but instead sounding annoyed.

She stepped inside and pulled the door shut behind her. "Nasty weather out there," she commented, putting her umbrella on the mat and taking off her coat. "We've seen an increase in car accident victims today."

"Any as grumpy as me?" Tadhg asked, in an attempt to make a joke.

Lily grinned. "I don't think that's possible. There was a rude woman, but she calmed down once she had pain relief meds."

Tadhg smiled, and Lily's grin widened. "I brought you a present."

She handed him a carrier bag, and he took it cautiously. Aside from the shopping she'd bought him last time, he couldn't honestly remember the last time anyone had given him a gift.

He pulled the object out and his eyes filled with tears, but he didn't care if he was embarrassing himself.

"I figured you'd be having trouble carrying hot drinks to your chair, what with the crutches and everything. So I thought a travel mug would solve that."

Lily was busy straightening up the lounge, and was oblivious to his show of emotion. He quickly wiped his eyes with his t-shirt, and he managed to find his voice. "Yes, I have to admit, I haven't tried to for fear of spilling it everywhere. Thank you. I really appreciate it."

Lily nodded, looking a little emotional herself. "You're welcome. I'll sort the food out," she said, holding up a brown paper package, a little soggy from the rain. "And how about I go make us a cuppa?" Without waiting for a reply, she went to the kitchen to put the kettle on. "Anything good on the news lately? Must admit, I never watch it myself."

"Same old crap," Tadhg admitted. Since the accident, he didn't seem to enjoy watching it as much as he used to.

"Ready to watch something a bit more cheerful? I brought over some DVDs," Lily said, bringing him a cup of tea and setting a plateful of rice salad and chicken in front of him. He took a sip of the hot drink. Damn it, she really did make a heck of a good cup of tea.

"What kind of DVDs?" he asked. "I don't do rom-coms, chick flicks or stupid comedies."

Lily rolled her eyes and dug into her bag. "I kind of figured that. Here, choose one of these."

Tadhg considered the selection. He had to admit, she had good taste in films. Not that he was going to tell her that of course.

"This one is okay, I guess," he said, handing her one of his favourite films of all time.

"Awesome! That's my favourite," she said, taking it from him and going over to put it on.

For the next couple of hours, they sat side by side, eating and watching the film. Every time she laughed, Tadhg's heart lifted a little, and as he glanced sideways at her, he felt emotions that he didn't think he'd ever felt before in his life.

He'd never been very good with relationships. He found it too difficult to let anyone get too close. And anyone he had let get beyond his walls had ended up stabbing him in the back.

But Lily was an entirely different creature. Despite his attitude toward her, she still persisted in treating him with nothing but love and kindness.

No one had ever made him feel this kind of hopefulness before. No one had made his heart feel a glimmer of joy.

He tried to concentrate on the end of the film, but all he could think of was whether she felt anything for him at all, or whether it really was only a sense of duty that kept her coming back.

His gaze rested on the travel mug. Surely she didn't buy food and gifts for all of her patients?

"Penny for your thoughts," Lily said softly.

Tadhg looked up and realised that the film had finished, and that she was watching him watch the mug.

He shook his head. "I was just wondering if you do this for all your patients, or whether there was more to this situation than you're letting on."

Lily smiled. "No, this is the first time I've ever done anything like this for a patient. And as for there being any other reason, well, like I said before, I like you, Tadhg. And I wanted to get to know you better."

Tadhg nodded. "I like you too, Lily."

Her eyes widened a little, and she tilted her head to one side. "Do you like many people?" she asked softly.

"No," Tadhg said. "I can't think of anyone else I like."

Lily considered this for a moment. Then she shifted forward on the settee and leaned toward his armchair. "Would it be inappropriate to say that I like you a lot?" she asked.

Tadhg shook his head, his heart hammering like a bongo drum in his chest.

She leaned forward a little further, and Tadhg didn't move away. When her lips met his, Tadhg closed his eyes and felt as though he had finally come home.

Chapter Seventeen

"It's totally cool, I really don't mind sleeping on the sofa while your sister visits," Sherrie insisted.

"Are you sure?" Fin asked. "Because I would get her to sleep on the sofa, but I don't think she'd be able to sleep, and then she'd get grumpy, and then–"

"I'm positive. I'm completely grateful that you've allowed me to stay all this time, it's the least I can do."

"Okay, well, it's only for a few days, then she will be heading back to San Francisco again."

"It's cool, really. I will tidy up and sort things out before she gets here." Sherrie handed Fin a cup of coffee, as they performed their now seamless morning routine before work.

"I'm picking her up this evening," Fin said, taking a sip as he passed her a plate of pancakes.

Sherrie added the strawberries and handed the plate back to him. She added more strawberries to her own plate and they both sat at the dining table to eat.

Since their 'sick day' on the beach, neither of them had approached the subject of their kiss, and Sherrie got the feeling that they weren't likely to anytime soon either. She was certain now that they really weren't meant to be in a relationship. They were close friends and colleagues, but she couldn't see it being anything more than that.

They finished their food in silence, then rushed about getting ready before leaving the house and hopping into

Sherrie's car to go to work. They alternated cars each day, so that they kept both of them running. They had discussed having just one car between them, but her car was all she owned now, and it was her bit of freedom. Sherrie wasn't really willing to give that up.

The day passed in a blur of tweeting and posting videos and campaigns to their social media sites. They were working on a few programmes of awareness, and after a few hours, Sherrie found that she couldn't stomach looking at any more footage of suffering creatures. She wondered why it was that most people had to see something they hated before they would take action to protect and save animals. Why couldn't they just love the creatures enough to prevent the cruelty in the first place? She believed that all creatures had the right to live a happy, pain-free life. What gave anyone the right to cause such suffering?

"Are you ready? I can drop you home before picking up Angela from the station."

Sherrie looked up at Fin. "I'm more than ready, that would be great, I can start dinner for when you get back."

"Great, thanks."

Sherrie grabbed her things and they headed out to the car. Once back at the house, Sherrie hopped out and Fin switched to his car and immediately left for the station.

Sherrie hummed a tune to herself while she cut up the salad and prepared them a tasty vegan dinner. She'd been a vegetarian for years, but thanks to Fin's influence, had been vegan since moving in with him. His flatmate was a staunch meat-eater though. Sherrie thought he should watch some of the videos she'd seen, perhaps that would make him change his mind.

The food was nearly ready and Sherrie was just setting the table when she heard Fin pull up outside.

Seconds later, the front door opened, and Sherrie heard the voice of Fin and the softer female voice of his sister.

"Hi," she called out, washing her hands and wiping them

dry on the towel. "I'm Sher–"

The sight of the woman who walked into the room made her cut off short. The woman stared at her too.

"You okay, Sherrie?" Fin asked, looking from her to his sister and back. "Am I missing something? Do you two know each other?"

"You look so familiar," Sherrie said.

Angela nodded. "So do you." She stepped forward and offered a hand, and Sherrie shook it, still in a daze.

The feeling that this blonde, round-figured sister of her best friend was someone incredibly important to her was so strong, that it made her feel quite emotional.

To hide her feelings, she pulled her hand away after a second and busied herself with serving the bean burgers. Once they were all seated, Angela started asking loads of questions. She seemed to think they must have met before in this lifetime, but Sherrie wasn't so sure. It felt like the connection was so much deeper than that.

By the end of the meal, they had ascertained that they definitely hadn't met before. But the feeling of familiarity was so strong, Sherrie had to resist the urge to reach out to touch Angela's face.

She couldn't ever recall having feelings for another woman before, but the sight of her large blue eyes and soft features was making Sherrie's heart flutter in ways it never had before.

Afraid that her feelings were plainly clear on her face, she insisted on washing up and cleaning the kitchen to allow Fin and Angela to have a proper catch up.

When all the dishes were cleaned and put away, the counters were sparkling and even the floor had been swept, Sherrie couldn't put off joining them in the lounge any longer. She took in a tray of drinks and cookies, and settled on the sofa next to Fin.

Though she joined in when appropriate, Sherrie couldn't

remember a word of their conversation when she lay on the sofa later that night, trying to fall asleep. Why had this woman had such an effect on her? Who was she?

Light fell across her face and she sat up to see who was coming into the room.

"Sorry," Angela whispered, coming over to the sofa. "But I just couldn't sleep, I needed to talk to you."

Sherrie sat up and shifted over in her sleeping bag to make room for Angela to sit down.

"I was feeling the same way," she admitted. "Since the moment you walked through the door, I feel like I have questioned everything I know about my life. I feel like I know you so well, like I have known you for a long time. But we have never met, I don't understand."

"Do you believe in reincarnation?" Angela asked.

"I guess, I mean it makes sense to have lived before, I think."

"Have you come across the idea of Earth Angels?"

Sherrie shook her head. "No, what is that?"

Angela told her the idea of Angels, Faeries, Merpeople and Starpeople coming from their realms and planets to Earth to help with the Spiritual Awakening, and something stirred in Sherrie's heart.

"That feels so familiar," she said. "Am I an Earth Angel?"

"I think so. I think that you and Fin are Merpeople. Your passion for the oceans and all the creatures living there would point to that."

Sherrie smiled. "I've always loved mermaids. I always wanted to be one as a child. I even have tails that I can swim in."

Angela returned the smile. "You look like a mermaid," she said.

Sherrie blushed. "Thank you. What kind of Earth Angel are you?"

"I'm an Angel. We tend to have rounder figures and blonde hair." Angela shrugged. "Plus I'm totally useless at saying no to people and I look after everyone else before I look after myself."

"I have a few friends who fit that description," Sherrie said. "Wow, how have I not heard of this idea before? It's amazing. So do you think we feel like we know each other because we're both Earth Angels?"

"I think that may well be part of it. I think we met at the Earth Angel Training Academy where we trained to become human."

"The what-what academy?" Sherrie asked, intrigued. "I don't remember going to an academy?"

"Most Earth Angels don't. I only know because I came across the idea in a fictional book that was set in the Academy. I recognised it when I read the story, and after watching a few interviews with the author, I think that she knows it was based on truth too."

"This is bending my mind a little," Sherrie admitted. "I mean, to discover that I was a Mermaid in a past life, and that we met at an Academy where we trained to be human..." She shook her head. "It's a bit mind-blowing."

"Sorry, I guess I've had time to get used to the idea, it all seems completely normal to me now."

Sherrie smiled. "It's okay, I'm just trying to take it all in."

Angela nodded and started to say something, but then stopped herself.

"What?" Sherrie prompted. "It's okay, you can carry on bamboozling me, I don't mind."

"It's just that, there's another concept, one that goes hand in hand with the Earth Angel idea."

"Yes?" Sherrie prompted when Angela paused for a while.

"The idea is that the Earth Angels have Twin Flames that they are meant to reunite with in this lifetime."

Sherrie raised an eyebrow. "And what is a Twin Flame when it's at home?"

Angela laughed softly. "You've pretty much hit the nail on the head. A Twin Flame is the person that makes you feel as though you have come home."

"Like a soulmate?"

"Yes, only the connection is deeper, and the love you feel for them is unconditional."

Sherrie's mind was whirring in overtime. Was Angela really suggesting what she thought she was suggesting? But she wasn't a lesbian, she liked men, not women. But there was something different about the Angel sat next to her.

"Are you saying...?" Sherrie trailed off as she looked into Angela's eyes and saw the longing there.

"I don't know," Angela whispered. "But the moment I saw you I felt as though I had finally come home."

Without thinking about it, Sherrie found herself leaning in, and Angela leaned toward her. When their lips met, the combination of Angela's touch, her vanilla scent and her warmth wrapped around Sherrie like a blanket, and she sighed softly. Their kiss deepened and Sherrie found herself passionately kissing a woman she barely knew, that she had just met, who was her best friend's sister.

And all she knew for certain was that she didn't want to stop.

* * *

"Whose bright idea was this again?"

Josh grimaced at Maisy, who was laying across his lap, shifting around in her sleeping bag, trying to get comfortable on the thin cardboard boxes that covered the concrete.

"Yours?" he said, though he wasn't entirely sure. His bottom had gone to sleep at least an hour ago, and if it wasn't for her company, he knew he'd be feeling quite miserable right now. If they hadn't raised two hundred pounds in sponsorship money to spend a night on the streets, Josh would have been suggesting they go home.

"I don't think I'm going to get any sleep," Maisy said, wriggling into a sitting position. She leaned against Josh and he put his arm around her, hoping to combine their body heat. Though it was relatively mild, and he had worn his winter coat, since the sun had set an hour before, a chill had settled inside him.

The idea that some people spent months or even years living on the streets made him feel sad, incredulous and quite angry. He wasn't a very angry person, it took quite a lot to make him feel that way, but knowing that there was no logical reason why everyone in the country, or even on the planet shouldn't have a home, it made him angry.

"I can't imagine it either," Maisy said softly, her head on his shoulder. "If we're finding this unbearable for a single night, then it must take a really strong person to be able to do this for longer."

Josh had got used to Maisy reading his thoughts. There were occasions when he could sense hers too, though less often than she read his.

"But how can people just walk past, and not see us?" Josh asked, as yet another passer-by walked past without a glance. "We're one of them, human beings, people. We're all one, do they not get that?"

"Of course not," Maisy said. "People on Earth see themselves as separate from other people, separate from animals, plants, the earth and the rest of the Universe. They haven't any idea of some of the things we know."

"Every person you meet should be treated as one of your family," Josh said, feeling passionate about the idea. "Would you walk past your mum if she were sat on the street? Or your brother?"

"I'm with you," Maisy assured him. "I completely agree. I'm just not sure how we can get that across to others."

"I think people should definitely try this for a night though, just to see how incredibly uncomfortable it is," Josh said, shifting a little on the cardboard covered concrete, trying to get some feeling back in his legs. "Let's talk about happy things," Maisy said. "It might be the only way to get through the night."

"Okay," Josh said. "What do you want to talk about?"

After talking about her ideas for the future, Maisy finally fell asleep on Josh's shoulder, but he was unable to close his eyes and relax. Knowing that there were people around and that they were in public, he felt a strong protective urge and wanted to stay awake to make sure Maisy was safe.

Finally, the sky began to lighten and the street lights went off, and the bustle of people passing by got bigger.

After someone slammed their car door nearby, Maisy awoke with a start. Her eyes flew open, then she moved her body and let out a groan.

"Oh my goodness, I feel like I slept on concrete last night."

"You did," Josh said wearily, his eyes drooping.

"Did you sleep?" she asked, stretching her sore muscles.

Josh shook his head. "Didn't feel safe enough to sleep."

"You must be exhausted. Let's go to the soup kitchen to get something to eat. We did promise to go there so they'd know we made it."

"Okay." They both stood up, and lurched about as though drunk for a few minutes while their blood flow was restored to their legs. They rolled up their sleeping bags and picked up the few bits they'd taken with them, then stacked the cardboard neatly by the nearest bin.

They walked to the soup kitchen in silence, Josh was just too tired to speak. They reached the building and went inside to get some food. Josh was desperate for a hot cup of tea.

"Josh! Maisy! You made it! How did it go?"

Josh smiled wearily at their supervisor. "Knackered," he replied.

Ian laughed. "I bet. Sit yourselves down, we'll get you breakfast straight away."

"Thanks, Ian."

Once they had some food in front of them, they tucked in, and Josh began to warm up. They chatted with some of the other patrons they had come to know over the weeks, but Josh was feeling too tired to really participate. They left a little while later, promising to return with the fundraising money the following weekend. They headed to the bus stop and Josh turned to Maisy. "I'm going straight home to sleep, shall we meet up later?"

Maisy shook her head. "I think I need to sleep and maybe read a book. I'll call you though."

Josh nodded and yawned. "Sounds good."

He waited with her until her bus came, then waved her goodbye. Then he hopped on the next bus going near his home.

When he stepped through the door, his mother came rushing up to him.

"Where have you been? I thought you'd be back much earlier!"

Josh explained that they went to the soup kitchen first, then he allowed his mother to crush him in a bear hug before going to his room and collapsing on top of the covers.

He was asleep within seconds.

Chapter Eighteen

"It's looking good," Chad said, looking around the building. "Will be amazing when we get to hand the keys over to the new owners."

Helen smiled. "It still seems like such a basic structure, but then it's got to be better than the temporary housing they have at the moment."

"Definitely," Chad agreed.

"So do you fancy watching a movie tonight? I managed to find some DVDs."

Chad nodded, then looked around them quickly to make sure no one was watching before leaning in for a quick kiss. "Sounds great. I'll bring my laptop and snacks."

Helen kissed him again then turned away to continue her task. Though the work was no less strenuous, she had found that each back-breaking day had really strengthened her body and she now found that she quite enjoyed herself.

Of course, she was still pleased when the day came to a close and they all made their way back to the charity headquarters. She glanced up at the rickety structure and felt a strong sense of coming home, which made no sense at all, considering how far away she was from her real home.

She went straight up to her room to get washed and changed for dinner, then joined the rowdy table of volunteers for the evening meal.

She and Chad sat next to each other, hands resting on each

other's knees. As soon as they could, they escaped the banter and went up to Helen's room, where they settled on the bed with Chad's laptop and snacks.

Due to the limited choice of DVDs, the film was terrible and they soon abandoned it in favour of kissing. Though they'd been dating for a few weeks now, Helen was still holding back and taking things slowly. When she warded his hands off yet again, he whispered.

"Who knows what will happen tomorrow? Let's seize the day."

Her dream came crashing back to her then and she remembered her mother using the same words. She pulled away from Chad suddenly and rifled through her bedside table to find the paper where she'd written down the dream. There were the same words, in her untidy scrawl. She turned back to Chad who was looking at her in concern.

"Everything okay?" he asked.

"Yes," Helen replied, tucking the papers away. "You just reminded me of something I'd forgotten."

She kissed him deeply then, and took his hand and placed it on her waist. "Let's do it," she whispered, a deep longing stirring inside her, as though she'd opened a door she had sealed shut. "Make love to me."

Chad's eyes widened a little, but he nodded and slowly began to undress her. As she lost herself in the sensations of her skin touching his, she wondered why she had held off for so long. The feeling of coming home filled her again, and she lost herself in the blissful feeling.

"Be strong, sweetheart, be strong."

Helen looked up at her mum and blinked. One moment she had been falling asleep in Chad's arms, the next, she was standing in the mists again, talking to her mother.

"Be strong for what?" she asked, feeling a little impatient at the lack of information. "What's going to happen?"

"You'll get through it," her mum promised, ignoring her direct question. "Everything will be just fine, I promise."

Helen frowned, but before she could question her further, felt the ground shifting underneath her feet. "What the?" The ground shook more, and a loud rumbling noise filled her ears and shook her awake.

Her eyes flew open and she looked up just in time to see the ceiling falling down on them. She didn't even have time to scream.

Helen blinked and coughed as the dust filled her eyes and nose. In the gloom she could just about make out Chad's face beside hers. Somehow, the rubble had fallen around them, forming a cocoon. A very dusty, claustrophobic cocoon.

"Chad?" she whispered, shaking him a little. Her heart was thumping hard, and she feared the worst when he didn't stir. "Chad," she said louder, shaking him a little more insistently.

Moments later, she gasped in relief when his eyes opened. A low groan escaped from his lips. "What's going on?" he asked, coughing and choking on the dust.

"I think it was an earthquake," Helen said, trying to sit up but finding that the space was too small. She wondered how much rubble was piled on top of them and how stable their space was. Chad shifted around and then let out a howl of pain.

"What is it?" she asked, trying to check for the source of his discomfort.

"My side," he gasped. Helen blinked several times, trying to gain better night vision. She reached out to touch his chest, then ran her hand down his side but came to a stop when it hit a sharp object. She carefully felt it, and felt his skin around it, and her heart thudded hard when she realised that he was impaled. Her hand came away sticky and wet, and tears filled her eyes. "Try not to move," she whispered. "I'm going to try and apply some pressure to stop the bleeding."

Chad's eyes were wide in pain, but he nodded.

She pulled the pillowcase off her pillow, and attempted to stem the bleeding with it. But in the dim light could see it changing colour quite quickly.

She shifted closer to him, and stroked his face. "Everything's going to be fine," she whispered. "Just stay with me."

Chad nodded, but his eyes were closing, and his body was relaxing.

"Chad," she said, tapping his cheek lightly. "Stay awake with me. The rescue people will come soon, they'll get us out, okay?"

"Okay," Chad whispered, his eyes opening again. He looked deeply into her eyes and he smiled. "You're so beautiful," he whispered. "I'm so glad I met you."

"I'm glad I met you too," Helen replied, her eyes filling up again.

"I love you, more than the moon and the stars combined," Chad whispered, making Helen's tears fall. It was the first time either of them had uttered the words, and until their union just hours before, Helen hadn't been sure how she felt. But knew now.

"I love you too, that's why you have to stay with me, okay? Just stay awake."

She heard a noise then, of rubble shifting, and while praying that it wasn't the rest of the building about to collapse on them, she turned her face upwards and yelled out:

"Help! We're under here! Help!" she wished then that she'd learnt some of the local dialect, but she prayed that someone would hear her and come to their aid. She wasn't sure how much longer Chad could hold on.

She turned back to face him, and was relieved to see that his eyes were still open.

"Tell my family I love them, please?" he whispered. "Especially my brother. He's going to be devastated."

Helen shook her head. "You can tell them yourself. And then you can introduce me to them, because we're both getting out of here, do you understand me?"

"Okay," Chad whispered, a shiver rippling through his body. "I'm so cold, would you hold me?"

Helen shifted closer to him and tried to combine her body heat with his, to keep him warm, all the while trying to keep some pressure on his wound.

She was beginning to feel a little drowsy herself, but didn't intend to drift off to sleep.

"Under here!"

The shout close by startled Helen awake and she blinked, and rubbed her eyes, trying to clear them of dust. She reached out to touch Chad's face. His cheek was cold. She shook her head. "No, no, Chad, wake up, please wake up."

She patted his face and shook his shoulder gently, but even in the darkness, she could see that his spirit had already left. Tears streaming down her cheeks, she gasped for breath as the sobs took over. Suddenly a stream of torchlight beamed down and she looked up, blinking into the bright light, and beyond it, saw the familiar face of Reuben peering at her.

"Helen! Oh my god, are you okay? Wait there, we'll dig you out, okay? Got to go slowly, everything is so unstable."

Helen nodded, but she couldn't speak. She stroked Chad's face, and leaned forward to kiss his lips.

Minutes later, Reuben and some of the other volunteers had cleared a big enough gap to get Helen out. Once she moved forward, Reuben caught sight of Chad.

"Oh, thank god, Chad's room was completely demolished, we thought we'd lost him."

Helen shook her head. "He's gone," she choked out. She held up her blood-covered hand to the torchlight and pointed to Chad's side where the beam was protruding from his side.

Reuben sighed and bowed his head. "Let's get you out of there," he said, reaching in to help Helen out. She stepped out into the open, feeling exposed in her dirty baggy t-shirt.

"We can't leave him in there," she said, looking back to where Chad lay.

"We won't," Reuben promised. "But first, let's get you safely away from here." He took off his shirt and wrapped it around her, then led her carefully across the pile of bricks that was once the charity headquarters. Helen looked around her in horror, seeing torch-lit glimpses of people injured and crying. She was glad of the darkness, she didn't want to see too much more. Reuben led her to the building across the street, which had withstood the quake, and got her a drink and a blanket to wrap her in.

"I'm going back to get Chad out," he said. "Stay here, they'll take care of you okay? If you need to call home, they have a working phone here too."

Helen nodded, but all she could think about was the fact that the man she loved, the man she had made love to for the first time just a few hours before, was now dead.

* * *

"Julie?"

Julie looked up to see Greg approaching the bench where she sat by the pond. She smiled at him and shifted across to make room for him to sit.

"I'm worried about you," Greg said. "You've lost your spark."

Julie tried to smile, but it didn't quite reach her eyes. "I guess I am struggling."

"I'm sorry that you won't get to be with your Flame in this lifetime. Violet told me about your vision."

"He was beautiful," Julie whispered. "The love, the connection between us," she shook her head. "It was indescribable."

Greg nodded. "Accepting that you won't get to experience a relationship with him is difficult. The only thing I can say is that he's obviously gone away on a very important mission, and that you are here for a very important mission. Now that you are no longer patiently waiting, what are you going to do?"

Julie exhaled. "I did have the spark of an idea the other week, of what I could do."

"Yeah? What was it? If you don't mind me asking."

"I realised that people who are doing spiritual things aren't very good at promoting themselves, and I do think that their work should be reaching more people. So I was thinking of either being a PR person for spiritual businesses and people, or creating something, like a magazine or a website that promotes them."

Greg thought about it for a moment. "I think those ideas have a lot of potential, I know I would certainly be interested in getting help with marketing and promoting."

"Thanks, I think it could work too."

They were quiet for a moment, and Julie could hear the kids laughing as they played knights and dragons in the trees on the other side of the house.

"Violet wants to organise a Twin Flame event herself, and invite all our past participants of the retreats, as well as anyone interested in attending future retreats. Perhaps you could undertake the promotion for that, I know she would welcome the help."

Julie smiled, feeling a little bit of hope glimmer within her. She might not get to be with her own Twin Flame, but she would love to make sure as many other Flames were reunited as possible. "That sounds great."

Greg patted her knee. "Better get going, I'm on dinner duty tonight."

"Can I help?"

"Nah, enjoy the dragonflies and the lilies and the peace."

A scream of laughter came from the direction of the kids.

"Well, you know what I mean," Greg said with a laugh.

"Thank you," Julie said. She watched her friend get up and return to the house, then sighed. She needed to shake off her melancholy and focus on the fact that she had three beautiful, healthy children, she had amazing friends and she had an idea of something to do with her life.

"Hey."

Julie looked up to see Violet coming toward her this time.

"I feel like the queen," Julie joked. "Holding court."

Violet laughed. "Greg said he'd been out to see you. I was just sorting through some crystals to use in my healing session later, and I found one that I wanted to give to you."

Julie frowned and held out her hand to receive the crystal that Violet offered her. It was an oddly shaped cluster of brown pointed crystals.

"What is it?" Julie asked, feeling like she'd missed something.

"Aragonite," Violet said.

Julie's heart jumped at the sound of her Twin Flame's name. She closed her hand around the piece, and it felt as though it was heating up in her palm. She held it to her chest and closed her eyes for a moment.

"I hope it was okay to give it to you, I just thought it would help you keep your connection with him."

Julie nodded, and a single tear rolled down her cheek.

"Thank you," she said. "And I know that the pain I feel is just a human reaction to not being with him. My soul knows we are connected always."

Violet wrapped her arm around her, and Julie rested her head on her friend's shoulder.

"It's okay to react in a human way. It's what we're here for, after all. Just please know that you're never alone, my dear Old Soul. Never."

"Thank you," Julie whispered.

Chapter Nineteen

"I still can't quite wrap my head around it," Fin commented.

"There's plenty of time to get used to it, baby brother," Angela commented, as she squeezed Sherrie's hand.

"But I didn't have any idea you were a lesbian," he said to his sister. "And you just left your husband," he said to Sherrie. "Don't you think it's all a little confusing?"

Sherrie shrugged. "If you could feel the intense connection we share, you would realise that it really had very little to do with gender and the labels we put on sexuality, and more about an intense, unconditional love."

Angela smiled and leaned across to kiss her. "Nicely put," she said.

"Thanks," Sherrie replied.

Fin shook his head. "As long as you're both happy, it's totally cool with me, I guess it's just not something I understand."

"You may well do someday," Sherrie said.

"Maybe. But what I really don't understand, is why you feel the need to run off to go travelling together. How can you leave me all alone at Fishy Friends with no one to bug me all day?"

Sherrie grinned. "As much as I do enjoy doing that, it just feels like we need to explore, see a bit more of the world. It's something we've both been wanting to do. Besides, I've already told Henry I will keep up with the social media side, and I will report on any events I attend wherever we are. He seemed okay with that."

Fin sighed. "I guess I will just have to be okay with it too, then."

Sherrie reached across to pat his knee. "We won't be gone forever, and we'll keep in touch online."

Fin got up to put the kettle on, and Sherrie and Angela took the opportunity to kiss again. Sherrie really couldn't get enough of her kisses, and her vanilla scent.

They stopped before Fin returned to the lounge with a tray of mugs.

"Well, here's to an exciting, but safe, trip," Fin said, raising his mug. The two women raised theirs and they clinked them together.

"To new adventures," Angela said.

"To new adventures," Sherrie agreed.

*   *   *

Tadhg watched her sleeping, taking in every curve, every detail of her face, and imprinting it on his memory. He had already silenced the alarm, and just wanted to take this moment to appreciate her beauty.

"I can tell you're watching me," she murmured sleepily.

Tadhg smiled. "I'm not watching you, I'm admiring you."

Lily opened one eye and peered at him. "Is it really time to get up?"

"Yes, it is," Tadhg said with a sigh.

"Why aren't you excited?" Lily asked, eyes open now, and a frown on her face.

Tadhg was quiet for a moment. "I guess it's just a little scary," he admitted. "What if I can't do it?"

"There's nothing for you to fail at. You just have to get used to it. It will make such a huge difference. We'll be able to go out for walks, go out to dinner, and you won't have painful hands from the crutches anymore."

Tadhg sighed. "I know, I know."

"So what's the problem? Sometimes I think you just look for things to be grumpy about for no reason."

Tadhg smiled at her pout. "You might be right," he admitted. "It feels more natural to me to be pissed off than to be excited or happy."

"I think that might be the saddest thing I've ever heard," Lily declared, pulling back the covers and leaping out of bed. Tadhg admired her figure and wondered for the millionth time why on earth such a beautiful creature would want to be with such an ugly man like him.

"I can still feel you watching me," Lily sang as she waltzed off to the bathroom, completely naked.

Tadhg chuckled, and pulled himself up into a sitting position. He took his morning pain medication, though since Lily had started staying over, he found he needed a smaller dose than normal.

"Are you joining me or what?" Lily called out.

Tadhg heard the shower running and grabbed his crutch to pull himself up. "Coming," he called.

An hour and a half later, they were at the hospital, waiting to be called in to have his prosthetic leg fitting.

"I was thinking," Lily said. "We should go on holiday or something, once you've got your new leg and it's all cool."

Tadhg raised an eyebrow. "We've only been together five minutes," he protested. "Besides, I haven't been working, I've hardly got the cash to go away."

Lily sighed. "Just keep the possibility in mind. Besides, I've been working like crazy. I can afford for us to go somewhere for a few days."

Tadhg felt conflicting emotions clash within him. Though he appreciated her generosity, the idea of being cared for and treated to a holiday made him feel weak. He hated feeling weak.

"Mr Carmine?"

Lily helped Tadhg up from the uncomfortable plastic

chair, and they followed the nurse to the consultation room. Tadhg felt his stomach flutter anxiously, and Lily must have sensed it, because she squeezed his hand and smiled at him.

Though not a believer in God, he silently thanked him for sending him an Angel.

* * *

"I'm sorry, Maisy is too ill to volunteer today."

Josh frowned. "What's wrong with her?"

Maisy's mum sighed. "She's been unwell since you two did the fundraiser and slept outside all night. We thought it was just a cold, but it seems to be getting worse. We're taking her to the doctors today. She had glandular fever a while back, which means her immune system isn't very strong."

Josh's eyes widened. "She didn't tell me she was feeling ill. Can I come and see her please?"

"I don't know, let me go see if she's awake and up for it."

Josh nodded, then waited on the front doorstep until Maisy's mum came back.

"She's asleep right now, why don't you pop by a bit later?"

Josh's shoulders slumped, but he nodded. He didn't want to disturb her if she was resting. He said goodbye and walked slowly to the soup kitchen, not wanting to leave them short of volunteers.

"Hey, Josh, no Maisy today?"

"She's ill," Josh said, hanging up his coat in the back room then grabbing an apron.

"Oh dear," Irene said. "I do hope she'll be better soon."

Josh took his place next to the older lady and began to serve food.

"Me too," he said.

"Tell her we all send our regards next time you see her, won't you?"

"I will, thanks."

Luckily, the shift didn't require Josh to be fully mentally present, and he got through it whilst thinking of Maisy and how he could help her. He'd been reading up about Crystal Children, and about crystals and their healing properties. He decided to get some crystals and take them to her house and do a healing session with her.

He arrived back at her house later in the afternoon, this time with a pocketful of crystals and some flowers.

Maisy's dad answered the door, looking like he was just about to leave the house.

"Hi, I've come to see Maisy," Josh said, even though he figured that would be plainly obvious.

"She's in hospital," her dad said, sounding frantic. "She collapsed while at the doctors and they've rushed her in to A&E."

Trying to remain calm, Josh breathed deeply. "Are you going there now? Can I come with you?"

"Sure." Maisy's dad locked the front door behind him, then unlocked the car, and Josh jumped into the passenger seat.

Josh gripped onto a piece of rose quartz tightly, and for the duration of the journey prayed to the Angels to keep his Maisy safe.

When they arrived at the hospital, they went to A&E and were informed at the desk that she had been admitted, and was already on a ward. They followed the receptionist's instructions, and made their way through the maze of corridors. At the desk they asked again, and were directed to a side room.

Josh's heart was hammering in his chest when they opened the door and stepped inside.

"Oh, sweetheart," Maisy's dad said when he saw her. Josh peered around his side, and his heart dropped. She looked so pale, with her blonde hair splayed across the pillow, eyes closed, and breathing shallow. Josh approached one side of the bed, while Maisy's dad joined her mum on the other side. They held a quick whispered conversation while Josh focussed on

Maisy. He reached for her hand, and almost recoiled at the coolness of it.

He heard Maisy's mum say the word 'pneumonia' and his heart began racing again. He knew that it could be much more serious when someone had already had glandular fever. He sat on the plastic chair, and took several deep, calming breaths. He needed to be calm to be able to channel healing energy to her. He gripped the rose quartz in one hand, and her hand in the other. He called in the Angels to assist him, as well as his Crystal siblings, and quite quickly, he felt his hands heating up and the energy coursing through him. He appreciated that Maisy's parents didn't ask him what he was doing, or interrupt him while he allowed the energy through. He imagined it running through Maisy, healing the damage caused by their night on the streets, and returning her to her beautiful, healthy self.

He sat there for a good fifteen minutes, before he felt the energy receding, and he slowly opened his eyes to see Maisy staring at him.

"I could feel that," she whispered. "And I could hear the Angels whispering to me."

Josh smiled, pleased to see her awake and responsive, which he took to be a good sign.

"Sweetheart, how are you feeling?" her dad asked.

Maisy smiled wanly. "Tired."

"You should rest, we'll stay here with you though, okay?"

Maisy nodded slightly. She looked at Josh.

"I'm not going anywhere," he said.

Maisy closed her eyes, a smile on her face, and soon her breathing changed as she drifted to sleep.

Josh had meant what he said. Even if they tried to throw him out when visiting hours were over, he would refuse to leave. He wasn't going to leave Maisy's side until she was better again.

Chapter Twenty

"Are you sure you're up to this?"

Helen nodded. "I need to do this. Have you met his parents already?"

"Yes," Reuben said. "Just briefly, earlier. They got on the first flight out here, they understood that we needed to deal with the funeral quickly, it's just too crazy to keep bodies for too long here."

Hearing Chad being described as a 'body' was like a knife through Helen's heart. She nodded, and took a deep breath.

"Let's do this."

They left the temporary accommodation they were staying in, and made their way down the street to where Chad's parents and his brother were guests at a small hotel.

The earthquake hadn't been a very bad one, the magnitude was significantly smaller than the one in 2015, but it had been strong enough to topple a few buildings that weren't as stable as people had thought, like theirs.

They reached the hotel just as three people were coming down the steps, and when Helen saw them, she stopped suddenly, her hand flying to her mouth.

"Chad?" she whispered.

The man shook his head. "I'm Todd, Chad's twin brother."

Heart hammering in her chest, Helen tried to compose herself, but the uncanny resemblance he had to the man she had loved and lost merely days before had thrown her off balance.

"I hear you were a very good friend of Chad's," the woman said, holding her arms out to gather Helen into a hug. "I'm Patsy, Chad's mum."

Helen accepted the hug gratefully. "We were very good friends," she said. "And had just started dating too."

"Oh, sweetheart," Patsy said, holding her tightly. "I'm so sorry."

"I'm sorry too," Helen whispered into her shoulder. "He was an incredible guy, I just can't quite believe he's gone."

"Neither can we," Chad's father said as Helen stepped away. Her eyes caught Todd's again she couldn't believe just how identical he was to Chad. Though this version had very sore, red eyes, and a deep frown on his face.

"Shall we get going?" Reuben suggested softly. "They will be waiting for us."

The group fell into step and they walked to the river, where Chad's body had been enshrined in logs and wood, to be cremated. There were many other cremations happening all along the river, all victims of the latest quake.

Unfamiliar with the ritual, they just followed the guidance of the locals there, and they each tucked something in with him. Helen tucked in a poem that she'd written for him. She had intended to give it to him, but hadn't had the chance.

They all silently watched the funeral pyre, the flames shooting up, sparks flying into the evening air.

Helen did nothing to stop the tears flowing down her cheeks, and she felt an arm wrap around her. She leaned gratefully onto Reuben, and looked across to see Chad's family all holding onto each other too.

It had been such a surreal nightmare.

Within a matter of days, her world had turned from a dream to... this. She had called Maggie to let her know she was okay, and her friend had told her it was up to her if she stayed or went back to the UK. She wasn't afraid to stay in Nepal, but she didn't feel any pull to stay anymore. She was ready to go home.

Once Chad had been consumed by the flames, the group made their way back to the hotel, where they had a drink in his honour.

"I really can't get over how alike you are," Helen said to Todd.

He smiled. "He doesn't often tell people he has an identical twin, I always joke it's because he's afraid they will like me more than him."

Helen smiled. She liked Todd's sense of humour.

Todd sighed and his smile disappeared. "I had a bad feeling about this trip. And I tried to talk Chad out of coming, but he wouldn't listen. I wish I'd tried harder."

Helen shook her head and put her hand over his. "I may not have known him long, but I do know that he was very set in his opinion of things, and once he decides something, there's no changing his mind."

"Yeah that's him in a nutshell," Todd agreed. "Stubborn as a mule."

They fell quiet and sipped their drinks. Helen listened to the subdued chatter of the people in the bar. The earthquake had shaken people, literally and metaphorically. Their fear of aftershocks and perhaps another bigger earthquake was palpable.

She felt bad that she could escape it, that she didn't live there, wasn't stuck there, thanks to the fact that she'd managed to retrieve some of her belongings from the rubble, including her passport. Reuben hadn't been happy with her going back there, with it all being so unstable, but there were some photographs of her and Chad that she desperately wanted, as a reminder of that fact that they had met, that it had been real. That they had been madly in love.

A tear fell and hit the table, and Helen bowed her head. Her eyes were so sore already, but she just couldn't stop the salty river from flowing.

"Hey," Todd said, reaching out to touch her arm. "Are you okay?"

She shook her head. "No," she said, not looking up for fear of losing it completely if she saw a look of compassion or sympathy on the face so like the man she'd lost.

"Can I escort you back to where you're staying?" he asked gently.

Helen nodded, and drank the rest of her drink quickly before standing up, and saying goodnight to everyone. Chad's mother gave her another tight hug, and promised to see her the next day before they flew back to the States.

Todd held the door open for her, and she followed him out onto the quiet street.

She shivered in the cool evening air, and he immediately took off his sweater, wrapping it around her in an act of chivalry that reminded her so much of Chad, a wave of fresh tears began to fall.

"I wish we could have met in happier circumstances," Todd said when they reached the door of the guest house. "The last message I had from Chad was all about you, and how happy he was. I had hoped he would bring you back to the States so we could meet."

Helen smiled. "It's good to hear how happy he was. I was too." She thought for a moment. "Are you leaving early tomorrow? Would you like to see the project we were working on? It withstood the quake, and I think Chad would want you to see why he came out here, what he achieved with his time here."

"I would love that," Todd said. "We don't leave until the afternoon. Shall I meet you here at ten with my parents? I think they'd like to see it too."

"Ten is great," Helen said. "Thank you for walking me back, I hope you sleep okay." She gazed at his face for a moment, and tried to imprint the image of his smiling eyes into her mind, to replace the image of Chad's ghostly, spiritless face.

"Goodnight," Todd said.

"Goodnight," Helen echoed, before stepping through the door.

She went up to her room and got ready for bed as quickly as she could. She was desperate to sleep, so she could escape the nightmare into her dreams.

"Helen, my darling."

Helen blinked and saw her mother coming through the mist. The memory of her previous dream came rushing back to her and she gasped.

"You knew," she said. "You knew that Chad was going to die, that's what you meant by difficult times, and to be strong."

"I'm so, so sorry." Her mother pulled her into a hug and Helen melted into her embrace.

"I don't understand, why did he have to leave? I loved him, Mum. I really loved him. Now he's gone!"

"I know it seems that way, but you know that those who have passed over never really leave. I mean," she held Helen at arm's length. "We're having this conversation now, aren't we?"

Helen frowned. "Yes, I guess so. But where's Chad then? Why isn't he here right now?"

"My guess is that Chad is having to make a decision right now, about where he wishes to go next."

"He has a choice?"

"Of course, we always have a choice. Just like in life, you always have a choice. You can choose to let this event affect your life in a negative way, or you can choose to let it affect you in a positive way. It's entirely up to you."

"It doesn't feel like I've chosen to have my heart shattered by losing the man I loved. Why would I choose that?"

"Well, what have you learnt from it?"

Helen thought for a moment. "To live every day as fully as possible. To not take a single moment in the presence of someone you love for granted. And to have as much fun as possible."

"I would say that all of that is a pretty good reason for choosing this situation, wouldn't you?"

Helen sighed. "No, not really. Because I would give up everything right now for a chance to see Chad again."

"I know you would, my love. I would feel the same way."

When Helen awoke the next morning, she wiped the tears from her eyes and tried to commit her dream of her mother to her long-term memory. But it was already fading away.

When ten o'clock rolled around, Helen went to wait outside for Todd and his parents. She closed her eyes for a few minutes and enjoyed the morning sunshine on her face.

"Good morning."

She opened her eyes and smiled at the three of them as they approached. "It is a lovely morning," she agreed. "I hope you all got some sleep." Though they nodded, judging by the black circles under their eyes, they couldn't have really got enough rest.

Helen led the way to the building site where she and Chad had been working, and kept up a lively stream of chatter as she showed them around, making sure to point out all the parts of the project that Chad had done personally.

Just as they stepped through to another room, Helen had a split second warning of something falling from above, but she didn't have enough time to act or shout out before the stone fell and struck Todd on the head, knocking him to the ground.

She quickly looked up to check there was nothing else coming down, then knelt by his side. His parents walked into the room moments later and Patsy started screaming at the sight of the blood coming from her son's head. While her husband tried to calm her, Helen applied pressure to his head wound and moved him into the recovery position. Heart hammering as she chanted *'no, no, no'* in her mind, Helen patted his cheek lightly, and called his name, trying to bring him round, but he was completely unconscious.

"We need to get him to a doctor," she said to his parents, who were watching in horror. "Go to the main office, just down the street, third building on the left, and get them to call for an ambulance. Tell them we have a head injury, he's breathing but unconscious."

Todd's dad nodded, and rushed off to do just that. She turned to his mother.

"He's going to be okay," she said softly, in an attempt to convince herself as well. "I won't let you go home without him."

Patsy nodded, but the terror on her face remained. Helen couldn't imagine the pain of saying goodbye to one son one day, only to face losing a second son the next.

It felt like an eternity before help arrived, and all the while, Helen continued to try and revive Todd, with no success.

The doctor arrived, and soon Todd was loaded onto a stretcher, then taken out to the vehicle waiting outside. Helen followed them, but only his dad was allowed to travel with them. Helen ran back to where she was staying, and got Reuben, so that he could give her and Patsy a ride to the hospital.

The ramshackle building was a far cry from the hygienic white hospitals they were used to in the west, and though she had promised his mum Todd would be okay, Helen began to lose faith that she would be right.

After an hour of waiting in the noisy waiting room, a nurse finally came out and led them all to a bed where Todd lay, eyes closed and his head bandaged up, but otherwise looking well.

Helen went to his side, and took his hand in hers.

"Todd," she said. "Please wake up."

As if he'd heard, no sooner had she made her request, his eyes flew open, and he blinked several times. Helen sighed in relief, and Todd's mum started sobbing.

Todd's gaze rested on Helen, and she smiled at him. "Welcome back," she said.

"Helen?"

"Yes, that's right."

"Helen, it's me, it's Chad."

Helen frowned. "Todd, what are you talking about? A rock just fell on your head and knocked you out, but you're going to be okay."

"I know what happened. When Todd came to the Other Side, I was waiting for him. I asked if he wanted to stay, and he said yes, but only if I would come back here. To be with you. He said we were meant to be together, and it wasn't fair that we hadn't had enough time with each other."

Helen didn't know what to say. Was Chad's spirit really now in Todd's body? Was he really back? There was only one way to find out.

"What was the last thing you said to me before you died?" she whispered.

"I love you," he said. "More than the moon and stars combined."

* * *

"So, I've created the posters and images to share online, and I've compiled a mailing list for the invites, and everything is set to go in the next couple of days."

Julie looked over her laptop to Violet, who was sat opposite her at the dining table. It had taken Julie a little while to get herself together, but plans for the Twin Flame event were now in full flow. She still carried the piece of Aragonite in her pocket, to remind herself that her mission was important, and that she had to continue on Earth, even though at times she really didn't feel like it.

"Perfect," Violet said. "I really can't wait to bring together all of the Twin Flames who have met here at the retreat over the years, it will be interesting to hear their stories."

"It's great that we're holding the event on the blue moon," Julie said. "I think it will create an amazing energy around it. After all, a Twin Flame connection is thought to only happen once in a blue moon, right?"

Violet chuckled. "Yes, though currently I think there have

been way more Twin Flame reunions than there have been blue moons."

Julie smiled. "It seems so."

"You know, Tim will be coming to the party. Have you guys been in touch at all?"

Julie frowned at Violet's overly casual tone of voice, and wondered what the Old Soul was implying.

"No, we haven't kept in touch, why?"

"Oh, no reason," Violet said unconvincingly. "I just thought you two had made friends after the mediation, and that you might have exchanged numbers or something."

Julie shifted uncomfortably. "Are you trying to set us up?" she asked.

"Set who up?" Greg asked as he passed through the room on his way to the kitchen.

"I think Violet is trying to set me up with your friend Tim," Julie called after him, making Violet blush. "Your recently bereaved friend," she added.

Violet held her hands up. "Okay, okay, I'm sorry. It's just that he mentioned to me how lovely you were, and how he wished he could have stayed a little longer to get to know you better."

"Seriously?" Julie bit her lip. She had enjoyed his company, and she had appreciated his compassion and conversation after she realised that she wouldn't be with her Flame. But have a relationship with him? She guessed it made sense, seeing as he had lost his Flame too.

Deep in thought, she didn't even notice Violet staring at her with a knowing smile on her face.

"I'll get the kettle on," she said with a smirk.

Julie sighed and shook her head, trying to bring herself back to the present moment and focus on the job at hand.

A couple of hours later, Julie stretched and yawned. "I think I need to get outside for a bit, it's far too beautiful a day to be cooped up inside."

"You're right," Violet said, closing her laptop. "Let's go

for a walk down to the river. We'll be back before the kids need picking up."

Julie nodded and the two women headed for the door, pulling on their shoes on the way out. Violet called over to Greg who was weeding the veg garden to say they were going for a walk.

"I really can't thank you and Greg enough for having me and the kids to stay here for so long. I feel bad that I haven't organised something else yet. The divorce and house sale is taking a lot longer than I imagined, and you have both been so patient and generous."

Violet smiled at her. "It really has been our pleasure. It's lovely to have the kids around, and it's great to have some female company too. In between the retreats it can feel a bit isolated when it's just me and Greg."

"It's so beautiful here though," Julie said, looking through the trees to see a squirrel darting from branch to branch. "It really feels like my soul needed to rest and recharge, and to be away from the world for a while."

"This is definitely the perfect place to do that," Violet agreed.

They kept up a steady pace down the hill, and soon found themselves at the bottom by the river. Thanks to the sunshine, the river was a hive of activity with canoes and kayaks full of people going past.

The two women sat down on the tiny beach, and Julie breathed deeply, closing her eyes to take in the sound of the water rushing past.

Despite the calm, she was thinking about Tim. Could a relationship with him really work? He had been great with the kids, and seemed like a wonderful man, but was there chemistry there? Was she attracted to him? In contrast to her encounter with her Twin Flame, their interactions seemed dull and lifeless. But then perhaps that was something that Julie would have to get used to.

"Penny for them," Violet said.

Julie sighed. "I was thinking about having a relationship with someone other than my Flame, and what that might look like. I guess, it would be similar to what I had with my husband. I mean, we did love each other, but the connection we had was very much above the surface, and quite superficial." She looked sideways at her friend. "Do you think it's possible to have anything deeper with someone who is not your Flame?"

Violet thought for a moment, and stared out at the ripples in the water caused by the low-hanging branches, dipping into the river.

"I think that in some ways, to know that you won't be with your Flame is quite freeing. That you can have a relationship with a man, and if it ended, it wouldn't have the potential to destroy you. And that you won't have such an intense connection that you will be distracted from your mission and not live up to your full potential." Violet sighed, and Julie stayed silent, considering her words.

"But," Violet said, "I must admit, even saying all of that, the idea of having to have a normal relationship, as secure and solid and as stable as it might be, really doesn't sound that amazing in comparison to the deep and unconditional love you can experience with your Flame."

Julie appreciated her friend's honesty, but in truth, her words really stung. She breathed in deeply and called upon Mother Earth to send healing through the sand underneath her to her heart. "Tell me honestly, if you were in my position, what would you do?"

Violet smiled at her. "If I were in the position where I knew I would never be with my Flame, what would I do?"

Julie nodded and still smiling, Violet shook her head.

"I'd probably walk into the sea fully clothed, and just keep walking until the waves pulled me under."

Julie nodded. "It does feel as though I'm drowning," she whispered.

"But the difference is, you still have such strong reasons

to keep going. Three very beautiful, strong reasons. You and your children are going to make such a difference to this planet, and all the people on it."

Tears began to fall but Julie smiled through them. "Thank you."

"Just telling you the truth, my sweet Old Soul. Now, what do you say we go pick those amazing kids up and we do something fun tonight?"

Julie nodded and got to her feet, dusting the sand off her jeans. "Sounds like a plan."

Violet got up too, and she held out a pebble to Julie. "Before we go, I want you to infuse this stone with all your fears, all your worries, all your frustrations, and I want you to throw it into the river, and allow it all to be washed away."

Julie accepted the pebble, and for a moment, held it tightly in her palm. Then she took a deep breath, opened her eyes and threw it into the centre of the river.

"How do you feel?" Violet asked, linking her arm in Julie's as they set off up the hill.

"Lighter," Julie said. "Much, much lighter. Thank you."

"Anytime."

Chapter Twenty-one

"Do you think we could include the UK in our travel plan? Say maybe for January?"

Sherrie looked at Angela who was sat across from her at the dining table and she shivered. "The UK in January? Are you insane? We're Californians, I'm pretty sure that might actually kill us."

Angela giggled. "True, the timing isn't great, but I just got this email," she waved her smartphone at Sherrie. "And there's an event that I would just love to go to in the UK on the thirty-first of January. I really think you would love it too."

"It's a long way to go to an event, what is it?"

"It's a Twin Flame party, and it's being held by a lady called Violet who is one of my favourite authors."

"I still haven't read her book. Isn't that the one you told me about when we first met? About Mermaids and Angels?"

"Yes, it is. I'll lend you my copy of the book," Angela said. "So it's possible? To attend the event?"

"I don't see why not, after all, if I've learnt anything from recent events it's that anything truly is possible, and that it seems silly to say no or never to anything."

"I completely agree," Angela said. "I couldn't possibly have dreamed that I would meet you and that we would be heading to Europe to travel."

Sherrie smiled. "I guess it's true what they say, the Universe works in mysterious ways."

"Yes, she does," Angela said.

*   *   *

"What do you mean, I should quit my art course?" Josh looked at Maisy incredulously as the credits rolled slowly up his TV screen in front of them.

"Don't get me wrong, you're a great artist, but you have amazing channelling powers. You should be healing and channelling. I mean, without you, I really don't know if I would have pulled through last month. I could hear the Angels calling me and everything. I was pretty close to going home, and you caught hold of me and pulled me back. That's pretty incredible, if you ask me." Maisy crossed her arms to make her point, making Josh smile.

He picked up the remote and switched the TV off, then turned to her and gave her his full attention. "What should I be doing then? Healing courses? I wouldn't even know where to start."

"I think it would be more beneficial to find a mentor. Someone already doing the work, someone you respect. Ask if you can learn from them, then practice on people, and build it up gradually. All of the amazing healers I have read about don't have reams of qualifications, they just have an innate ability and have learnt along the way."

"And you think I could be like them," Josh said, feeling the truth in the words.

"Yes. You are an Awakened Crystal Child. You can channel the healing power of the crystals on Earth and of our siblings in the Crystal World. The ability to do that effectively is rare, believe me, I have been Awake longer than you and I have still not yet managed to channel it as well as you can."

Josh blushed. "Stop it, you're going to give me a big head," he protested.

"I'm not saying all of this to boost your ego," Maisy said, rolling her eyes. "I'm saying this because I think it will take far too long for you to realise it all by yourself, and that you need to come to this realisation quickly."

Josh smiled at her blunt words. He loved how she always said what she meant, always spoke the truth.

"Anyway, before your ego does get completely inflated, I have a suggestion, somewhere for us to go together next year to finally celebrate my birthday."

Josh raised his eyebrows. "Oh, where?"

"Violet is holding a Twin Flame party, and she has invited everyone on her mailing list, which I signed up to months ago. It's for everyone who has attended her retreats, met their Flame or who is looking for their Flame. I want to go."

"To see if your Flame is there?" Josh joked.

Maisy punched him lightly on the arm. "No, silly. I would like to meet her and also talk to other Earth Angels. I mean, think about it, a whole party full of people who understand us? It will be amazing."

"Okay, sounds good. And hey, I should have a car by then, I could even drive us."

Maisy's eyes widened in mock horror and he laughed. "Hey," he said. "I'm a good driver. I'll get us there safely."

Maisy grinned to show she was kidding. "I know. I trust you with my life, you know that." She leaned against his arm and he breathed in the scent of her hair.

"Yeah, I know," he said. "I trust you with mine too."

* * *

"I know we haven't known each other for very long, and this may seem completely sudden and out of the blue, but," Tadhg very slowly lowered himself to the grass on his good knee, and Lily's hands flew to her mouth when she realised what he was about to do.

"Lily, you have seen me at my worst, you have loved me and nurtured me regardless, and you have changed my entire perspective and outlook on life, and to be honest, brought me back from the dead. For that, you have my eternal gratitude, and I would love to spend the rest of my life with you, and to love you and support you in the way that you have loved me and supported me. So, Lily," he pulled a small box out of his pocket and Lily started to cry.

"Would you do me the honour of marrying me?"

Tadhg's heart was hammering so loud in his chest that he only just heard the tiny 'yes' that she uttered behind her hands. When he didn't move, she took her hands away and nodded. "Yes!" she cried out. She held out her hands to help him back to his feet, and he took the ring from the box, and slid it onto her finger. Then he leaned in and kissed her softly.

"I love you, Lily."

"I love you too, Tadhg," Lily said, staring into his eyes. She looked down at the ring and shook her head. "I had no idea you were planning this today. When you suggested a picnic at the park, I just assumed you wanted an excuse to eat brie and crackers and yell at kids for being too noisy."

Tadhg laughed, and his laughter scared away a couple of ducks at the edge of the pond. "I must admit, I was looking forward to doing those things too," he joked. He shook his head. "I kind of can't believe you said yes. Why would you want to spend your life with a miserable old fool like me?"

Lily reached up to kiss him again. "Hey, you're not allowed to get cold feet immediately after popping the question. And besides, you're really not as miserable as you once were."

"True," Tadhg said as they settled back onto their blanket. He watched Lily admiring her ring glinting in the sunlight as she got some more food out of the plastic bag that was acting as their picnic hamper.

"Also, I think we might be Twin Flames," she added casually, handing him the brie and a knife.

Tadhg frowned. Though he didn't know what that was, the words resonated deeply within him, almost feeling like a key sliding into the perfect lock.

"Twin Flames?" he questioned, taking the cheese.

"Yeah. I've been reading up about them recently, and the description just feels like it makes sense. I've signed up to a mailing list to find out more. I can show you some information about it if you want."

Tadhg shrugged. "Sure." He frowned. "Is being Twin Flames a good thing?"

Lily chuckled. "I hope so." She bit into a cracker covered in hummus, and crunched it thoughtfully while still staring down at her ring. She looked up at Tadhg and smiled. "I guess we'll find out, won't we?"

Chapter Twenty-two

"I can't believe today has come so quickly," Julie said, shivering a little as she got in the car.

Violet started the engine and quickly put the heater on. "I know, it's just zoomed by. I only hope that we've got everything ready."

"I think we've thought of everything," Julie assured her, hoping that it was true. "Time to just enjoy the party now."

They set off down the lane, heading to the village hall they'd rented for the Twin Flame party. They had spent the previous two days decorating it, and Julie thought it looked amazing. The kids were visiting their dad, so she had been free to focus purely on the event, which had made things a little easier.

Ten minutes later, they pulled up outside, and got out of the car, both shivering as the brisk January air tried to get through their layers of warm clothing.

"Hi, Lucy!" Violet called out to the lady from the village shop who was catering the event.

"Hi, Violet! Everything is ready, shall we get in there and set up?"

Violet nodded. "Yes please, we're just doing a few finishing touches, the guests will be arriving in an hour or so."

Lucy nodded then returned to her car and started to unload, directing the two teenagers she had with her.

"Let's get this lot inside," Violet said to Julie who was pulling boxes of cups and paper plates out of the boot of the car.

They finished setting up, and Julie looked around the hall, admiring their handiwork. She took a few photos on her phone, and promised herself she'd take more photos later so she could use them to get further work in organising events and doing promotions.

"Hello, Old Soul."

Julie turned around and came face to face with Tim. She smiled at him. "Hello yourself, Starperson," she said. "How are you?"

Tim hugged her and kissed her on the cheek and she felt herself blush a little at the contact.

"Good," he said. "Much better than the last time I saw you. I feel as though I'm finally beginning to move on."

"That's great," Julie said, fiddling with the name badges. "You're a bit early, are you planning to speak tonight?" she asked.

Tim shook his head. "No, I don't think it would be helpful to other Twin Flames for me to speak. After all, tonight is about uplifting them and bringing them hope. How will my story give anyone hope?"

"Because you got through it," Julie said, reaching out to touch his arm. "There might be other people attending who have also lost their Flames, who need to hear that it is possible to survive the loss."

Tim sighed. "I don't know, I'll see I guess."

"Okay, well I'd better just finish off a few things, can I catch up with you later?"

"Sure," Tim said, moving over to where they were already setting out the food.

Julie watched him go and smiled. By the end of the night, she was going to ask him out. She was ready to move on, too.

The next hour passed by in a blur, and soon the hall was teeming with people, some of whom were dancing to the local band that Julie had hired.

She checked her watch then checked the badge table. It looked like everyone who had pre-booked had arrived, so it was time to get Violet up on the tiny stage to welcome the guests.

She made her way through the crowd of people and found Violet chatting to a group of women. She politely tapped Violet on the shoulder and she stopped mid-sentence and smiled at Julie. She excused herself then followed Julie to the stage.

"No matter how many times I get up on stage, I still have strong déjà vu from when I used to do this in the Academy," Violet said to Julie, adjusting her purple velvet dress.

Julie smiled. "I bet. Well, let's get this party started." She took a deep breath and went up on the stage and tapped the microphone gently. The sound quietened the noisy crowd and brought all eyes to where she stood in the spotlight.

"Welcome, Twin Flames! Thank you so much for coming out on this chilly winter's evening to celebrate both the blue moon and the reunion of so many Flames. I would like to introduce you to our beautiful host, Violet. She is a speaker, teacher, author, Old Soul and runs the Twin Flame Retreat."

Julie stepped back and Violet stepped onto the stage and up to the microphone to the cheers of the audience.

Julie stepped off the stage as Violet thanked everyone for coming and then launched into talking about how the reunion of the Flames was going to change the course of the world. Then she invited anyone who had put their name down at the door to speak to come to the side of the stage.

A small group of people made their way toward Julie, and she got everyone lined up for their chance to speak and share their stories. Each person would only have ten minutes, so she planned to time them, then give them a signal when they had one minute left. She ushered the first person onto the stage, a young woman called Helen.

* * *

"My name is Helen," she began, gripping onto the microphone so that her hands would stop shaking as the whole hall of people stared up at her. "And I met my Twin Flame while we were both volunteering in Nepal last year. We were there building homes for those who had lost theirs during the 2015 earthquakes, but while we were out there, another earthquake happened and the building we were staying in collapsed on top of us."

There was a collective gasp, and tears came to Helen's eyes as the memory of Chad being impaled by the rubble flashed through her mind.

"We were trapped there for a while," Helen continued. "And it was while waiting to be rescued that I finally realised just how much I loved him, and that we were meant to be together. Before we were found, however, his injuries became too much, and he slipped away."

Tears were streaming down Helen's cheeks now, and she could see others in the audience wiping their eyes. Though she had practiced what she would say a few times, it was still difficult to talk about her experience. Despite her overwhelming emotions, she continued, determined to share her story.

She reached the part about Chad returning into Todd's body, and another gasp went around the room. Helen saw the lady on the side of the stage signal to her that she had one minute left and she nodded slightly.

She held her hand out, and Chad joined her from the side of the stage. "I felt it was important to share our story, to show that no matter what the situation, even when it seems impossible to be with your Flame, that it is possible to be reunited, just hold onto your faith and it will be so. Thank you."

Helen left the stage to a huge round of applause and cheers from the audience, and once back on the ground she reached up to wrap her arms around her Flame and kiss him hard.

"I'm so glad you came back to me," she whispered.

"Of course I came back," he said. "We're meant to be together."

"Yes," Helen agreed. "We are."

She took his hand and they re-joined the audience, who were already listening to the story of the next person on stage.

"Helen."

Helen turned to see Maggie behind her and she released Chad's hand to throw her arms around her friend.

"Maggie! It's so good to see you!" Helen pulled away and looked at Maggie's companion. Her eyes widened. "Steve?"

"I have been dying to tell you, but I wanted to tell you in person," Maggie said, trying to keep her voice low enough so not to disturb the rest of the crowd. "Steve came for a reading after he returned from Australia and we realised very quickly that we were Twin Flames. It was his chocolate brownies that did it."

Helen's eyes widened further and she grinned. "That's incredible! I'm so, so pleased for you both." She hugged her friend again, then hugged Steve too. She realised then that she felt no attraction to Steve whatsoever. She wondered if she had felt a connection to him because she was meant to introduce him to Maggie.

"I wanted to thank you," Steve said. "If you hadn't given me Maggie's number, we might never have found each other."

Helen smiled. "You're very welcome."

"That was an amazing story, by the way," Steve added. "Goes to show how powerful the Twin Flame connection is, to even be able to bring you back from the dead."

Chad nodded. "Yes. And though I wish my brother could still be here too, he was adamant that his own Flame was already waiting for him in the Angelic Realm and that I should take his place on Earth so I could be with Helen."

"Amazing," Maggie said. Her gaze shifted to the left slightly, and Helen recognised that she was receiving a message.

"Todd is very pleased that it worked," she said with a smile. "And he's also very pleased that you will be naming your son after him."

Helen's hand flew to her stomach in shock. "How did you know?" she asked without thinking. "We haven't told anyone yet."

Maggie smiled. "I know everything, remember?" she said jokingly. "Seriously though, congratulations. He's going to be a beautiful Crystal Child, I can see him now."

Helen's eyes filled with tears. "Thank you." She leaned into Chad's side and he wrapped his arm around her. At that moment, the crowd around them erupted into applause and their attention was drawn back to the stage where a red-haired woman was taking the microphone.

* * *

What the hell was she doing on a stage in front of a room full of people? She must be crazy. She caught Angela's eye, and took a deep breath, and focussed on her Flame's face.

"Just a few months ago, I left my husband, after I realised that not only did I have no feelings for him anymore, but also that he was trying to hold me back from my mission on this planet." Sherrie took another deep breath and smiled. "I was staying with a work colleague, when his sister came to stay. When she walked into the room it was like I had been struck by lightning. I knew her. Instantly. And when we came into contact with one another, it was as though I had finally come home," her voice broke a little and she was a little embarrassed to find herself overcome with the memory of the emotions she'd felt that day.

She looked around the room and saw many people nodding in agreement with her words.

"Before that moment, the idea of being with a woman had never entered my mind as a possibility. I wasn't a lesbian, I had never fancied women before. But when I met Angela, gender no longer had any importance. I loved this soul, this woman who stood before me, and I knew that my life would never be the same again."

She caught Angela's eye and her Flame gave her the thumbs up. She took yet another deep breath, and gathered the courage to do what she needed to.

"There's something I haven't told my Flame yet though, something pretty major, and I figured that right now would be the best time to say it."

Sherrie saw the smile slip from Angela's face and a worried frown replace it. She beckoned for her to join her, and slowly, Angela made her way up to her side.

"Angela," Sherrie said, "I know we haven't been together very long, but I know that I want to spend as much of my human time with you as possible." She got down on one knee and pulled a tiny pouch out of her pocket. She slid the ring out of the pouch and held it up to her Flame, who had her hands over her mouth and tears streaming down her cheeks.

"Will you marry me?"

There was a hushed pause as everyone in the audience waited for Angela's response.

When she finally said yes, the whole hall erupted.

Sherrie didn't even notice the noise. As she slid the ring on Angela's finger and then stood up to kiss her, the only thing she noticed was the way her lips felt pressed on hers, and the vanilla scent that reminded her so much of home.

* * *

"We should be up there sharing our story," Lily whispered to Tadhg as they listened to another Twin Flame couple recounting their tale of how they met, then were separated for ten years before meeting again. "Our story is pretty awesome, you know."

Tadhg shifted uncomfortably on his prosthetic leg. He

needed to sit down soon.

"I don't really like being in the limelight," he said, aware that his tone was a bit grumpy. "I'd rather just listen to everyone else."

"That's cool," Lily said. "Shall we sit down for a bit? I'm feeling a bit tired and I really want to dance once the stories are over."

Tadhg knew that she wasn't really tired, and that she was just picking up on his discomfort. He leaned down to kiss her, taking her by surprise. "Okay, let's sit down for a bit," he said, playing along. They made their way over to some chairs and tables set up along the outside wall, but before they could sit down, Tadhg felt a hand on his shoulder. He turned around and saw a woman grinning at him.

"Tartan! It *is* you!"

Tadhg frowned, and looked at Lily who looked bemused.

"I'm sorry, I think you have the wrong person," Tadhg said.

The woman shook her head. "No, I would recognise you from anywhere. My name is Amy, but at the Earth Angel Training Academy, my name was Athena, and I was the Professor of Free Will. You were called Tartan and were the Professor of Human Culture."

Tadhg was still frowning, but Amy's words were resonating with him and chinking into long-forgotten parts of his mind.

"I think she might be right, Tadhg," Lily said. She waved to the stage where Violet stood off to the side, listening to the soul speaking. "I read her book, and you do seem incredibly like the Professor of Human Culture. For a start, he was a really miserable sod."

Tadhg and Amy laughed.

"Really?" Tadhg said. "I'm in her book?"

"We both are," Amy said. "And I'm sure your Faerie friend here may well be in it too."

"You can tell I'm a Faerie?" Lily asked, delighted. "I've

only recently figured that out myself." She held out her hand. "Lily. Pleased to meet you Amy, also known as Athena. Goodness, head of all the Guardian Angels, I feel like I should curtsey or something."

Amy laughed loudly, and a few people looked round as if to hush her. She held up her hands in apology. "No need to curtsey," she stage-whispered to Lily. "I'm quite the normal person, I promise."

"Normal?" the man stood next to her scoffed. "In what dimension?"

Amy grinned at her companion, and introduced him to Tadhg and Lily. "This is my Flame, Nick. We met at Violet and Greg's wedding."

Lily smiled. "Nice to meet you, Nick. This is Tadhg, by the way, we just recently got engaged."

Nick shook Tadhg's hand. "Congratulations to both of you."

"Thank you," Tadhg said, his mind still whirling from all the new information. Could he really have been a professor in an Academy in his last life? As bizarre as it sounded, it felt very real.

"Seems crazy, doesn't it? All of these people here, talking about their experiences of meeting their Flames, and talking about the changes happening in the world. Makes me hopeful that the Golden Age may yet come to pass," Amy said.

"I don't see why it can't," Lily said. "So many people are waking up, realising that there is more to life, so much more to experience, to learn, to remember."

"But there's still so much hate in the world," Tadhg said. "There's still war, poverty, disease, and crime. Do you really think it's possible to eradicate all of that? I don't."

Lily and Amy looked at each other and nodded.

"Yup," Lily said. "He's definitely Tartan."

She and Amy burst out giggling and this time, they were hushed and told to be quiet. While they attempted to calm themselves, Tadhg turned back to watch the stage, feeling a little disgruntled, yet amused at the same time.

He hated to admit it, but he had a tiny flicker of hope that the future would be brighter than it currently looked. Lily slid her hand into his and he gripped it tightly as he smiled down at her.

And he knew exactly who to thank for that flicker.

Chapter Twenty-three

"My name is Josh, and this is Maisy."

Josh gripped Maisy's hand nervously, and looked at the faces in the audience, all of whom looked welcoming and friendly.

"We weren't going to speak tonight, but when we realised that we were the youngest ones here, we felt it was important to say something. We're Crystal Children, and we have memories of our world, and of being at the school on the Other Side. Partly thanks to Violet's book, so thank you Violet."

Violet smiled and nodded at him from where she stood at the side of the stage.

Josh was aware that he was recounting their story for the audience gathered before them, but all he could think about was the feeling of Maisy's warm hand in his. He told them about her near-death experience, and then he looked down at Maisy and smiled. "It was in that moment, when I thought that Maisy might have left me and gone home, that I knew our connection was so much more than I had realised, and that we were Twin Flames." Maisy's eyes widened, as he hadn't told her of his revelation.

Josh breathed deeply, feeling a little more confident and sure of himself now that the audience were being attentive, though the giggles coming from the back were slightly unnerving.

"I read a lot about Twin Flames after that. All of the information was varied and though not all of it applied to us, there was something that stood out. And that was that being with your Flame was like being home. Their smell, their touch, their smile, it is all created to make us feel like we have come home. When I read this over and over, I realised that I felt exactly like that around Maisy, and I also realised that was why it pained me to see homeless people on the streets. Because they had nowhere or no one to call home." Josh could see a few people in the front row getting a bit emotional, and he struggled to keep his composure.

"I suppose what I wanted to share was this idea I had, of why the Twin Flames are reuniting right now. Being on Earth is hard for Earth Angels and the Children of the Golden Age, because we know that our original homes are so much more beautiful and peaceful and lovely than Earth. And we have this longing, this pull to leave here and go home. I know that many have done so, and we've heard a lot of amazing stories tonight of some who have left and come back. So I think that Twin Flames are reuniting right now, to help Earth Angels to feel at home here, to provide them with a place, a person to connect to so deeply, that they can bear to weather the storms that come with being human."

Josh smiled at Maisy, and saw her eyes were glistening with unshed tears. "I hope that if you are here tonight without your Flame, that you one day find your way home again."

*   *   *

Julie listened to Josh's words with tears in her eyes. She looked around the audience, trying to spot Tim. She needed to tell him tonight that she liked him, and that she would like to get to know him better. They may not be Twin Flames, but she felt like she would feel at home in his arms.

Once Josh had stepped off the stage with Maisy to a round of applause, Julie signalled to Violet that he was the last to speak. Good thing too, it was getting quite late and she had promised the band a second set.

"Is it too late to speak?"

Julie turned around to see a beautiful young woman with bright blue eyes and dark curly hair, dressed in a dark blue dress. She checked her watch quickly.

"You would have five minutes max," Julie said. "We're running behind already."

The woman smiled. "I only need five minutes."

Julie nodded and waved to get Violet's attention, as she thanked all of those who had shared their stories. Violet saw her and Julie motioned for the woman to step up onto the stage.

"Looks like we have one more soul who would like to share her story," Violet said, stepping back from the microphone.

The woman thanked her and stepped up to front to speak.

Julie was too busy scanning the crowd again for Tim to notice the woman's words, but then something she said grabbed her attention.

"We'd been together for literally only a few hours before I was in an accident, and was paralysed from the waist down, and brain damaged so I could no longer speak. My Flame stayed with me the whole time, and cared for me for many months. But then I made a mistake with my medication, and it killed me."

She paused and Julie realised her mouth was wide open. The story was so familiar, but surely it couldn't be?

"When I crossed over, I was assured that I would get a chance to return to Earth, that my mission was not over yet. And so, here I am. I became a walk-in, and I have come here tonight, because I'm very much hoping that my Flame is here in the room." Tears ran down her cheeks, making Julie want to cry too.

"I'm hoping that he will recognise me, and that he will forgive me for leaving him," she concluded, her voice breaking.

Julie saw movement in the audience, and when she saw Tim step toward the stage, a look of wonder on his face, her heart dropped to her feet.

"Hannah?" he whispered, staring up at the beautiful, crying woman. She nodded and he jumped up onto the stage, and reached out for her. She stepped forward into his embrace and they kissed.

Julie allowed the tears to fall freely. Though she was upset that she had begun to feel something for a man that was never destined to be hers, to see Tim reunited with his Flame when it seemed like there was no possibility of them ever being together again, gave her hope.

She felt the piece of aragonite in her pocket and smiled. Maybe one day, she too, would find her way home to her Flame.

About the Author

Michelle lives in England, and when not creating new worlds and characters, she helps other Indie Authors with their own publishing adventures. She also loves to photograph wild things, like deer and mushrooms, and has recently fallen in love with Instagram. She loves baking cakes and chatting with friends, though probably spends too much time chatting and not quite enough time working!

Please check out her other books in the Visionary Collection, and stay tuned for more books coming very soon.

Please do write a review of this book on **Amazon**, every review helps! Michelle loves to get direct feedback, so if you would like to contact her, please e-mail **theamethystangel@hotmail.co.uk** or keep up to date by following her blog – **twinflameblog.com**. You can also follow her on Twitter **@themiraclemuse** or 'like' her page on **Facebook**.

To sign up to her mailing list, visit: **michellegordon.co.uk**

The Earth Angel Series:

The Earth Angel Training Academy *(book 1)*

Velvet is an Old Soul, and the Head of the Earth Angel Training Academy on the Other Side. Her mission is to train and send Angels, Faeries, Merpeople and Starpeople to Earth to Awaken the humans.

The dramatic shift in consciousness on Earth means that the Golden Age is now a possibility. But it will only happen if the Twin Flames are reunited, and the Indigo, Crystal and Rainbow Children come to Earth, to spread their love, light and wisdom.

While dealing with all the many changes, Velvet struggles to see the bigger picture. When she is reunited with her Flame for the first time in many lifetimes, her determination and resolve to fulfil her mission falter...

The Earth Angel Awakening *(book 2)*

'No matter how overcast the sky, the stars continue to shine. We just have to be patient enough to wait for clouds to lift.'

Twenty-five years after leaving the Earth Angel Training Academy to be born on Earth as a human, Velvet (now known on Earth as Violet) is beginning to Awaken. But when she repeatedly ignores her dreams and intuition, she misses the opportunity to be with her Twin Flame, Laguz. Without the long-awaited reunion with her Twin Flame, can Violet possibly Awaken fully, and help to bring the world into the elusive Golden Age?

The Other Side (of The Earth Angel Training Academy) *(book 3)*

Mikey is an ordinary boy who just happens to talk to the Faeries at the bottom of his garden. So when an Angel visits him in his dream and tells him he must return to the Earth Angel Training Academy in order to save the world, despite his fears, he understands and accepts the task.

Starlight is the Angel of Destiny. By carefully orchestrating events at the Academy and on Earth, she can make sure that everything works out the way that it should, even though it may not make sense to those around her.

Leon is a Faerie Seer. He arrives at the Academy as a trainee, but through his visions he realises that his role in the Awakening is far more important than he ever imagined.

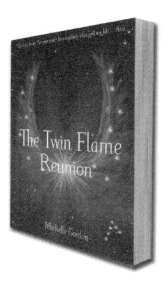

The Twin Flame Reunion *(book 4)*

Greg and Violet are among many other Earth Angels who are reuniting with their Twin Flames. They must work through their own fears in order to be together, but at times, it's just too overwhelming.

Aria and Linen left the Other Side hand in hand, to become humans on Earth. Despite being afraid of forgetting everything, Aria's memory remains intact. But when she finds Linen, he has no memory of her at all.

Charlie experiences an Awakening, and meets his Twin Flame. But when he is unable to control his anger, he changes his future forever.

Starlight leaves her Twin Flame on the Other Side, and goes to Earth, so she can assist Violet and the other Earth Angels with the Awakening. But she is not prepared for everything that comes with being human.

Leona has a vision of her Twin Flame, and decides to search for her. But when they find each other, Leona can See that it may not last.

The Twin Flame Retreat *(book 5)*

A lost Starperson, an out-of-control Faerie, a lonely Angel and an Indigo searching for love all attend the Twin Flame Retreat, which is now owned by Violet and Greg.

The three days they spend in the woods will change their lives forever.

Visionary Collection:

Heaven dot com

When Christina goes into hospital for the final time, and knows that she is about to lose her battle with cancer, she asks her boyfriend, James, to help her deliver messages to her family and friends after she has gone.

She also asks him to do something for her, but she dies before he can make it happen, and he finds it difficult to forgive himself.

After her death, her messages are received by her loved ones, and the impact her words have will change their lives forever.

The Doorway to PAM

Natalie is an ordinary girl who has lost her way. There is nothing particularly special about her or her life. She has no exceptional abilities. She hasn't achieved anything miraculous. Her life has very little meaning to it.

Evelyn is the caretaker at Pam's. The alternate dimension where souls at their lowest point find the answers they need to turn their lives around. The dimension dreamers visit, to help people while they sleep.

One ordinary girl, one extraordinary woman.

One fated meeting that will change lives.

The Elphite

Ellie's life is just one long, bad case of déjà vu. She has lived her life before - a hundred times before - and she remembers each and every lifetime.

Each time, she has changed things, but has never managed to change the ending.

This time, in this life, she hopes that it will be different. So she makes the biggest change of all - she tries to avoid meeting him.

Her soulmate. The love of her life.

Because maybe if they don't meet, she can finally change her destiny.

But fate has other ideas...

I'm Here

When Marielle finds out that a guy she had a crush on in school has passed away, the strange occurrences of the previous week begin to make sense. She suspects that he is trying to give her a message from the other side, and so opens up to communicate with him, She has no idea that by doing so, she will be forming a bond so strong, that life as she knows it will forever be changed.

Nathan assumed that when he died, he would move on, and continue his spiritual journey. But instead he finds himself drawn to a girl that he once knew. The more he watches her, and gets to know her, he realises that he was drawn to her for a reason, and that once he knows what that is, he will be able to change his destiny.

Earth Angel Sanctuary

A safe space to Learn, Grow, Heal and Evolve.

The Earth Angel Sanctuary is an online space where Earth Angels can watch videos on the 'basics' to shifting emotions with advanced energy clearings, rituals, interviews plus so much more, all to help Earth Angels help themselves.

Founded by Sarah Rebecca Vine in 2014, the Earth Angel Sanctuary has several contributors and has new videos and information added to it every month.

To join simply visit:

earthangelsanctuary.com

You can sign up for a monthly or yearly membership.

In gratitude for the nourishing vibrational energy of the trees that have sustained me for so many years, I have created:

Sacred Tree Spirit

In this dream-like space, you can receive vibrational therapies and core-belief re-programming to improve emotional and physical health.
You can relax in the healing crystal spa, watch life-affirming films in the imaginarium, attend courses and purchase unique handmade gifts in the backcountry homestore.

I look forward to connecting with you!

sacred-tree-spirit.com

designs from a
different planet

madappledesigns
.co.uk

Peace of Stone

Harmony for Heart & Home...

In our Shop
Gifts ♥ Crystals ♥ Jewellery ♥ Incense
♥ Essential Oils ♥ Angels ♥ Books

Like us on [f] or follow Peace of Stone on [t]
keep updated on upcoming events and exclusive offers

Tel: 01600 714303 E-mail: peaceofstone@hotmail.co.uk

www.peaceofstone.com

Zenith

Crystals ♥ Jewellery ♥ Books
Ethical & Fair Trade Gifts
Readings ♥ Talks ♥ Workshops

16a Corn Square, Leominster, Hereford,
Herefordshire

01568 613145

Mon - Fri: 10:00–17:00
Sat: 10:00–16:00

This book was published by The Amethyst Angel.

A selection of books bought to publication by The Amethyst Angel. To view more of our published books visit **theamethystangel.com**

We have a selection of publishing packages available or we can tailor a package to suit each author's individual needs and budget. We also run workshops for groups and individuals on 'How to publish' your own books.

For more information on Independent publishing packages and workshops offered by The Amethyst Angel, please visit **theamethystangel.com**

Manufactured by Amazon.ca
Bolton, ON